A WOLF'S TREASURE

THE KINCAID WEREWOLVES #5

L.E. WILSON

EVERBLOOD
PUBLISHING

ALSO BY L.E. WILSON

<u>Deathless Night Series (The Vampires)</u>

A Vampire Bewitched

A Vampire's Vengeance

A Vampire Possessed

A Vampire Betrayed

A Vampire's Submission

A Vampire's Choice

<u>The Kincaid Werewolves (The Werewolves)</u>

Lone Wolf's Claim

A Wolf's Honor

The Alpha's Redemption

A Wolf's Promise

A Wolf's Treasure

The Alpha's Surrender

<u>The Sergones Coven (Dragon Shifters & Vampires)</u>

Fire of the Dreki

Blood of the Master

THANK YOU NEW PATRONS!

Thank you to my new patrons on Patreon!

Aileen V.
Cheryl M.
Sharon P.

Your support means so, so much to me. I truly couldn't do this without you.
Much love,
L.E.

CHAPTER 1

Duncan's blood raced, burning through his veins with a shot of fear, a spark of excitement, and a twinge of longing, though he hadn't felt any of those things in a very long time.

She was stalking him.

The lass with the dark curls. The one he'd seen that day he was with Lucian.

The wee lass was stalking a werewolf.

A wide grin split his face as he lathered his jaw and neck for a shave. It would do him no good to meet her properly for the first time with a day's worth of whiskers. He rinsed his hands and wet his razor, then began scraping the stubble from his left cheek.

As he shaved, he thought back to the first time he'd noticed he was being trailed. After everything had been sorted out with Lucian and Keelin, Duncan had decided to give the pup a little bit of space. Lucian was maturing nicely, and thanks to his new mate, that explosive temper of his was finally cooling to a simmer.

Of course, he—Duncan—had helped with that by annoying Lucian on a regular basis for years until he no longer had such a hair trigger. Not that he would ever receive any thanks for it.

But he was digressing.

Unlike Lucian, Duncan didn't feel the need to run wild every night. Older than the pup by many years—though a wee bit younger than Cedric, the almighty alpha—he was quite comfortable in his skin. And around humans.

What he did love to do, was dance. Country dancing, to be precise. Something his pack mates probably weren't aware of. Not because he was hiding it, but because they were a bunch of self-centered bastards when it came to their free time, preferring to spend it with their Faerie mates than with him.

All except Cedric. But as the alpha, he'd made it very clear long ago that he preferred to spend his downtime alone with his Guinness beer and the latest Netflix series he was binge watching.

Duncan had taken an interest after meeting Keegan when he'd come up from Texas. That alpha knew his way around a Two-Step, and Duncan had been immediately romanced by the music and etiquette of the dances—the Two Step, the Waltz, Swing, Line Dance...hell, even the Polka. He'd taken a few free lessons, watched some videos on YouTube, and now made it a point to sweep the lasses off their feet at least twice a week. Three times, if he could manage to sneak away. Human lasses loved nothing more than a male who could swing them around a dance floor.

And this was how he'd found out he was being followed by the lass in the forest. The one he'd never thought to see again.

All had been quiet on the Faerie front for a few days, so with his alpha's permission to take a break from patrols, he'd climbed into Vina—his Jeep—and headed south to a nightclub he often frequented called Risky Business. Or maybe it was Risky Boys. Risky Beers? No, that couldn't be right. Duncan stopped shaving and thought about it a moment. The name really didn't matter, though, so he shrugged and continued with his task.

What did matter, was that he was being followed.

At first, it had been nothing more than a tickle on the back of his neck one night when he was at the club. Like the tip of a feather barely sliding over his skin. But over the next few hours, as he'd hit the dance floor with a few lasses he saw there on a regular basis, that tickle had become a scratch. And by the time he'd finally left the club, sweating his arse off and jonesing for a cheeseburger smothered with bacon, that scratch had begun to burn until his hackles rose in warning. As he'd weaved his way the few blocks to his Jeep, Duncan had glanced around, all casual-like, trying to pinpoint the source.

She hadn't bothered to hide when he'd spotted her down the street. Hadn't even attempted to stay out of his sight. Instead, she'd stood with her wee booted feet planted right in the middle of the sidewalk, arms crossed beneath full breasts that made his mouth water with the urge to bite into something other than a burger.

The force of that hunger had taken him so unawares, his knees had weakened and he'd nearly stumbled.

Her head had tilted to the side in a curious pose as she'd watched him falter, and Duncan had been struck anew by the luxurious look of the dark curls falling loosely over her shoulder.

Pausing with his hand on the door handle of his Jeep, he'd stared back, too dumbstruck by the oddness of the situation to think straight.

He knew those curls. He'd seen them before.

After a few seconds, her arms had dropped back to her sides. With a bored look, she'd turned and wandered all leisurely-like into the alley beside the dance hall.

Unsure of what to do, Duncan had stared at the spot where she'd last stood. Should he follow the lass? Get in Vina and go home? Had he really seen her or had one of his dance partners dropped something in his whiskey when he wasn't looking?

The possibilities were endless.

In the end, he'd gotten into his Jeep and headed home, convinced he'd imagined the entire situation. But mostly because he was fookin' "knackered", as his vampire friend, Aiden, would say, and just wanted to eat and get some sleep.

However, over the next few weeks, as he'd run patrols around the diameter of Cedric's territory and went about other menial daily tasks, the lass had appeared another sixteen times.

And Duncan no longer thought she was only in his imagination.

The lass would appear out of nowhere, sitting up high on a branch in the forest as he ran beneath in his wolf form, swinging her legs without a care in the world as she watched him go by. She'd watch him walk in and out of his apartments. He'd even caught her staring blatantly in windows. Always watching. Never saying a word.

As he didn't discern any type of a threat from the situation, Duncan went about his business as usual until one day, feeling a bit crabbit and weary of her spying, he'd attempted to speak to her.

He'd walked out of the grocery store to find her a few spaces away from Vina, head cocked at a curious angle, dark eyes serious as she'd studied his every move like he was some sort of alien creature. His steps had faltered when he noticed her there, but only for a moment.

Opening the back of his Jeep, he'd put his bags inside. "Sexy grin" in place—the one that never failed to bring the females running—he'd turned to say something charming and perhaps slightly teasing. Something that would bring a smile to her face and a light to her eyes.

But when he'd met her steady stare, whatever he'd been about to say had melted like sugar on his tongue. At some point, he'd finally managed to stutter out an awkward greeting, but even that had taken the majority of his brain power. He couldn't even remember now what it was he'd said. But it must've been something especially *glaikit*, for the lass had looked at him like he was the village idiot before she'd turned and meandered away with not a whiff of urgency, as always. Her full hips had swayed back and forth with a natural swagger, causing a startling growl of need to rumble in his chest.

Och, aye. *That,* he could remember.

Over time, Duncan had come to the conclusion there was one reason and one reason only for his impaired reaction to this particular lass after he'd spent hundreds of years wrapping females around his finger—or at least not offending them by his presence.

She was *more.*

And as to why she'd been following him around these past weeks? Well, that was quite simple to see. This lass was not normally attracted to males, and yet, she found herself irresistibly attracted to one now. It was the only explanation that made sense.

She obviously had a strange fascination with him. Perhaps she was confused by her feelings and was trying to puzzle it out, and this is why she kept appearing everywhere he was, she was trying to figure out why she was so very attracted to him.

It made perfect sense, and the only reason he could think of for her strange behavior.

Duncan rinsed the remaining lather from his face and checked to make sure he hadn't missed anything. He slapped on a little smelly stuff—females loved the smelly stuff—and went to his room to finish getting dressed.

It took him a minute to decide what she would like him to wear, but ultimately settled on jeans and a thin, green sweater that brought out the color in his eyes. Tonight, he was going to talk to the lass. Really talk to her without tripping all over his words...or his own feet. Tell her why he believed she was so taken by him, and they could finally stop dancing around each other, and he could get on with his life.

Alone.

Duncan wasn't a "love 'em and leave 'em" kind of male. For reasons beyond his control, he was just a "leave 'em". And he tried not to dwell on the reasons behind it. If he did, being in this world would be too lonely, indeed.

So, he was off to meet his mysterious lass. But first, he needed to stop by Cedric's apartment for a quick briefing.

Duncan arrived at Cedric's door at the same time as Marc, the pack mate he was the fondest of, though he would never tell the others such a thing as they would be devastated.

The alpha's voice came to them through the door, raised in anger. "Have ye lost yer wits, ye crazy fool?"

Another voice, quiet and refined, answered, "I haven't had them in some time now, wolf. It's one of the best things about living to be as ancient as I am."

Duncan and Marc shared a look before Duncan opened the door and announced their presence. "What's all th'—" His words were cut short as he strode out of the foyer and into the apartment proper and saw who Cedric was speaking to.

Prince Nada, aka the Faerie prince, was there, sitting in Cedric's favorite chair. His long, silver hair hung loose down his back, and he wore his usual fancy suit. Black, this time. Though on occasion he would go with all white. One hand rested on the silver head of his ever-present cane. Though he seemed to carry it more for appearance, since Duncan had never actually seen him use it to walk.

Cedric paced back and forth in front of him, wearing a path in his new area rug between the couch and the window. Brock was already there sitting on the couch, as was Lucian, the two of them in almost identical poses with their heavy arms crossed over their wide chests. Lucian wore his usual severe expression, but Brock was watching the scene playing out before him with a look of amusement sparkling in his blue eyes.

"What's going on?" Duncan asked his pack leader.

The prince stood from his chair and announced in a stage whisper, "I think your leader is having some sort of breakdown."

"I'm no' having a breakdown!"

Duncan studied the male he'd known for more years than he could count. His cheeks were ruddy with temper, his eyes were flashing white sparks, and he could hear the scrape of his teeth grinding together. If Cedric kept this up, he would have no way to chew his meat to nourish himself. "Och, Cedric. Dinna let him get tae ye. Ye ken he only says what he says tae rile ye up."

Cedric shook his head. "Ye dinna hear, Duncan. The prince has a plan."

"Oh, yes!" The prince smiled. "I just thought of it this

morning. And thought I would flash on over here to tell you about it."

The grin on Brock's face grew. "And it's a helluva plan. Just wait till you hear."

"Is anyone goin' tae tell us this 'plan'? Or are ye going tae leave us standing here like a couple o' fools?" Marc asked.

"It does no' matter, because I'm no' going tae do it," Cedric growled.

"But it will fix all of our problems."

"No." Cedric pointed at the prince. "It will fix yer problems. No' mine. It will only give me more!"

The prince rolled his eyes. "I do think you're being overdramatic. Princess Duana is—how do you wolves say it—quite a 'bonnie lass'. You could do much, much worse."

Duncan looked from one to the other. "What in the god's green earth are ye two talkin' aboot?"

With a great, heavy sigh, Cedric ran his hands over his head, smoothing back his ponytail, which had, in fact, become quite askew. "Th' daft prince has come up with th' perfect way tae distract Duana from her obsession with 'curing' th' soul suckers." His chest heaved with another intake of air, which he blew out slowly before he said, "He wants me tae mate with th' lass."

The prince grinned at everyone in the room in turn. "It's a brilliant idea. I'm so glad Cedric thought of it."

"I dinna think o' it, ye fool. Ye did!"

Duncan buckled beneath the force of the alpha's temper, as did the rest of the wolves.

"You don't have to shout," the prince told him pleasantly.

"I may be old, but I can hear you just fine."

A low growl rumbled from Cedric's chest, and he took a step toward the Faerie prince.

Acting fast, and as the only one in the room who'd been with his alpha long enough to get away with it, Cedric leapt between them just as Brock and Lucian jumped to their feet. Whether to run or to back up their alpha, he didn't know, but one move would've been just as smart as the other.

He didn't dare lay a hand on Cedric, as it very well might get bitten off. Quite literally. But he did manage to catch his white eyes with his own. "I dinna think chewing up th' prince is a good idea, Cedric."

He flashed his canines. "Yer wrong. Tis th' best idea I've had in a long time."

Duncan felt a heavy weight settle on his right shoulder, and he caught a whiff of something sweet and pleasant. Lavender? Tearing his eyes from his alpha's, he turned his head slightly to find the prince's chin resting on his shoulder. The smile was still on his face. The one that made him look like he was off his head.

"You do know I'm quite capable of taking care of myself," he whispered in Duncan's ear.

"Ye have no' seen a wolf like my alpha when his temper is roused," he responded.

The prince came around to stand beside him, never taking his eyes from Cedric. His head tilted to the side as he studied the alpha's face and form. "That's where you're wrong, young pup. Quite, quite wrong."

Duncan frowned, his hackles beginning to rise. He was

not young. Nor was he a pup. And he was about to remind the prince of that fact when a flash of color in Prince Nada's eyes distracted him. He blinked. Looked again. But the illusion was gone.

Cedric pushed him out of the way, snarled at the prince, then abruptly turned on his heel and stomped away. They all let out a collective breath as the weight of his anger lifted from their backs.

Duncan however, continued to stare at the prince as a sense of unease crawled over his skin. But there was no sign of rainbows in his eyes.

Perhaps he'd only imagined it. Or, perhaps it was a trick of the Fae. Either way, there was no need for his heart to be thumping the way it was.

Prince Nada gave him a wink, then retrieved his cane from where it rested against the side of the chair. In a rare moment of mental clarity, he said, "Think about my proposal, wolf. We need to get Duana under control, and who better to do that than you? And we both know why."

Duncan exchanged a look of surprise with Marc just as Cedric whirled around with a growl.

But the prince was gone.

"Fookin' Faeries!" Cedric shouted to the space where the prince had stood. Then he grabbed the chair he'd recently vacated and flung it across the room, where it smashed against the fireplace.

Brock and Lucian ran over and began to pull the larger pieces from the fire before they set the whole building ablaze.

Cedric saw what they were doing and roared, "Get out! Get out! All o' ye!" He pointed at Duncan, white eyes glowing through the strands of hair that had been ripped from his ponytail. "Except ye, Duncan. Ye stay here with me."

The others filed out, nearly tripping over each other in their haste to get out of the way of Cedric's wrath.

Duncan watched them go, trying not to laugh. They should all know by now that Cedric was a fair and level-headed alpha. Well, maybe not Brock. He'd only just joined the pack a short time ago. But the rest of them should know; Cedric wouldn't take out his anger on his pack. Not unless they'd caused it.

It was one of the reasons Duncan chose to stay with him.

"Ye owe them both an apology, for talkin' like that aboot their mates," he said.

"I was no' cursing their lasses, I was speaking aboot th' prince."

"Aye, but still."

Cedric glared at him a moment, but then the anger faded from his eyes. He sighed heavily. "Aye, I will."

"What do ye need from me?" Duncan asked. Cedric would have a plan. He always had a plan. Because there was no way in hell he could ever see his alpha giving in to the prince's crazy idea. Cedric would never marry one such as Duana. The lass was bonnie, for sure, but she was *an olc*—a Dark Fae. They had fought side by side to remove her kind from this world. And although a few of them—like Duana and Marc's Bronaugh—had been missed and were as sane as the *la maithe* tribe the prince ruled over, it didn't mean anything. She would turn, as would Bronaugh. It was inevitable, and Duncan wasn't looking forward to the grief his brother would feel when she did.

Hands on his hips, Cedric just stared at him for a good long while. Finally, he took another deep breath, the last of the tension falling from his shoulders and the glow leaving his eyes. "Och. I dinna ken," he said.

"How aboot a beer?" He, himself, sure as hell could use one.

"Aye. Thank ye, Duncan."

He got two bottles from the fridge, popped off the caps, and brought one over to Cedric.

"What th' fook am I supposed tae sit on now?" he asked Duncan as he took the bottle without taking his eyes from the pile of smashed wood and blue material of his favorite chair.

"Th' couch is good and comfy," Duncan told him.

"Aye, but it's no' my chair."

"Then maybe ye should no' have smashed it."

Cedric grunted and took a drink. "Twas that or lose me shit completely. And it's a wee bit early for the humans tae be seeing a black wolf running through their halls."

"And that's why I keep telling ye tae only rent out the spare apartments in our building tae fellow shifters."

Those white-blue eyes shifted over to Duncan. "Ye may be right, Duncan. But I dinna ken if I could live around more o' ye. I have enough on my hands just dealing with ye four."

"At least it was ye who broke yer furniture this time, and no' us." Duncan grinned. He and the others had crashed through Cedric's furniture more than once when being a little too enthusiastic about leaving.

Cedric grunted, and took a long swallow from the bottle in his hand.

"So, what are ye goin' tae do?"

"Aboot?"

Duncan swung his arm out, nearly spilling his drink. "Aboot marryin' the princess! And the daft prince who came up with th' idea, tha's what!"

Cedric shrugged one thick shoulder.

A shock of surprise shot through him. "That's it? Dinna ye want tae get out of the prince's crosshairs?"

"Aye. But…" he drifted off, not finishing the thought.

"But?" Duncan repeated. "But what? The lass is *an olc*, Cedric. She carries th' dark magic within her. Ye canna seriously be thinking o' courting her!"

"Bronaugh is *an olc*."

"Bronaugh will turn, just like they all do."

"Haud yer wheesht, Duncan! Dinna say such a thing. Marc would be fookin' destroyed were anything tae happen tae th' lass!"

"It's going tae happen, Cedric. It's just a matter o' time."

"I thought ye liked her."

"I do! She's bonnie and braw. But that does no' change what's going tae happen in th' future. And then she will be like…" He paused. "Well, ye ken th' ones I mean."

Cedric gave him a stern stare. "She will no' become one

o' them, Duncan. Those Faeries are gone. Locked away with the sick ones."

"That's no' what Lucian and I saw when we found Duana at Keelin's house."

Cedric's gaze snapped to his. "Ye dinna tell him anything?"

"Och, no. O' course no'." Anger coursed through him. He couldn't believe this male, his friend, who'd fought by his side in the last war, who'd rescued him from the enemy, was giving serious thought to mating one such as Duana.

Or, perhaps it was just that if Cedric were mated, it would truly leave him all alone.

Cedric finished his beer in one long swallow and set the empty bottle on the mantle. Turning to Duncan, he put one large hand on his shoulder. It was heavier than the prince's head had been.

The weight was reassuring. The words he spoke, not so much.

"Ye canna go through th' rest o' yer life with no one tae rest yer head on, Duncan. Dinna ye have a lass in mind ye could be with?"

"I have a lot o' places tae rest my head, Cedric. A lot o' choices. And so do ye. Ye dinna need tae settle, because ye think it will bring aboot peace."

"I would no' be settling, my friend."

Duncan stared into his alpha's eyes, searching for the truth. And when he found it, the anger that filled him turned to sorrow. "Then ye will end up no different from me, Cedric. and for that, I'm verra sorry."

CHAPTER 2

Ryanne checked her hair in the bathroom mirror, peeking at her reflection between a small space left empty of the "You're beautiful" and "You're not alone" quotes written in different shades of lipstick. The humidity in this part of the country was wreaking absolute havoc on her curls. Making a face at her reflection, she pulled them into a ponytail high on the back of her head, leaving a few strands to fall softly around her cheeks, and taking care that the tips of her ears were covered.

This was the third night in a row she'd come to this silly club looking for the wolf. Honestly, she didn't know what the humans found so interesting about sliding around a dance floor in smooth-soled boots—the lack of traction made even worse by the sawdust all over the floor—to singers who whined about losing their girl, their truck, their dog, et cetera....et cetera...and how sad their lives were now.

She did, however, like the look of the human men in their tight jeans and hats. It was very reminiscent of the "Old West" and made her wonder how many of them could really ride a bull.

Or, could handle riding her.

Smiling at her own joke, she checked that her red blouse was tucked into her tight jeans, turning around to admire the bling on her ass. It could probably use some more. She had a lot of ass to cover.

She made a mental note to pick up a bedazzling kit at the store and went out into the club proper.

The overly loud twang of a guitar hit her full on as she left the ladies room, and Ryanne winced as her sensitive ears grew used to the volume. Once she had the various levels of sounds worked out, she made her way through the crowd, smiling at the cowboys and keeping one eye on the dance floor for the sight of the green-eyed shifter.

A werewolf who had moves without using his powerful jaws? It intrigued her to no end.

When she'd first seen him with the red-haired shifter in the woods behind the house where The Key lived, she'd been too surprised at first to hide. And by the way his mouth had dropped open, he had been shocked as well. But then she'd heard Duana, the princess, ordering her soldiers to search the pine-covered hillside. The threat of being found had been enough to boost her into action, and she'd taken off out of there. She couldn't be caught. Especially not by her.

Later, alone in the forest, she'd waited for the hunt to begin. The wolves would be after her, she was sure of it. But she wasn't frightened. No. She was looking forward to it. Evading them would be fun, as long as she didn't get too cocky and become dinner.

Imagine her surprise when no patrols were sent out. No great, furry beasts roamed through the trees, noses to the ground searching for her scent. No howls raised the hair on the back of her neck and shot exhilarating thrills across her skin.

He hadn't told them.

Or, he had, and they either didn't know who she was or didn't take her to be a threat.

That would be their first mistake.

Unable to set aside her curiosity, she'd hung around, hoping to find the green-eyed wolf and follow him. It had taken a while, but she'd finally run across him as he'd patrolled the forest just a few miles away from their first run in. Ryanne had followed him all night until he'd returned to his den, a small apartment building with many rooms his pack shared with others who were not of his species. Including the Fae.

A strange way for shifters to live.

But maybe they liked the thrill of being hidden in plain sight. Of living amongst those who would take them out in a heartbeat if they were discovered. And how did they disguise themselves from Faeries?

Ryanne thought perhaps she would like these wolves.

So, she'd waited and she'd watched, keeping well out of the sight and smelling distance of the others who lived there. And then one night, he'd climbed into a Jeep the color of the trees and left.

Ryanne had followed him. Though he'd driven fast, she found she could easily run behind. And when he'd hit the main road, she'd kept up with just a little more effort. In this way, she'd traveled with him all the way to this club.

Again, she'd watched and she'd waited, quickly picking up how to blend in with the other patrons so she could further study this wolf who lived with humans and Faeries. As someone who didn't want to be found, Ryanne tended to keep her distance from anywhere that drew large crowds.

He came here quite often, and for reasons she couldn't quite comprehend, was a big hit with the "ladies". She assumed it was because they considered him a good dancer, for it certainly wasn't his silver tongue. The one and only time he'd spoken to her, he'd tripped over his words so hard she'd had no idea what he'd been trying to say.

So, yes. He was a handsome male. But perhaps not very intelligent. Still, for some reason, she was intrigued.

After the first few times he'd come here, she'd stayed away from his home and the threats within. Instead, she frequented this place. Even on nights he didn't show, it amused her to watch the humans, and the bar was dark enough and large enough for her to make a quick escape if needed. Ryanne had never spent so much time around them before, and it was really quite fun. She knew how the world worked, for the most part. She just preferred to stay in her part of it and under the radar.

Sometimes, she even spoke to the more virile males and allowed them to buy her a gin and tonic, a drink she'd heard someone else order and discovered she liked a lot. She drew the line at shuffling around the dance floor, though. That was just silly. And besides, if she was out there, she wouldn't be able to hold down her spot at the bar where she now sat. The one that gave her a perfect view of both the entry door, the bathrooms, and the dance floor.

Right on cue, the door opened and in walked her shifter.

Ryanne smiled when she saw him, much to the consternation of the human man who was attempting to hold her attention.

As though he sensed her there, the shifter's bright green eyes darted around the room until they landed on her. They narrowed when he saw the man standing beside her chair, vying for her attention. And to Ryanne's surprise, he started heading in her direction, fists clenched at his side, before he caught himself and abruptly stopped. With a look of confusion, he shook his head, unclenched his hands, and made a beeline for the closest female. With a wink and a smile, he had her out on the dance floor.

Ryanne watched with interest, noting how his eyes kept finding her, and how he would pull the woman closer when he saw she was watching him.

The man beside her stepped into her line of vision, and she realized he was saying something. She raised one eyebrow in a silent question.

"I asked if you'd like another drink, or if maybe you'd just like to get out of here?" he asked her.

She took a good look at him for the first time. He was tall, and not bad looking with his dark hair and eyes. His skin was a light brown, and his teeth were straight. A bit on the thin side for her taste, but overall a rather attractive human. "And where would we go?" she asked him.

Scenting a conquest, he pressed closer to her and took one of her curls between his fingers. "Anywhere you'd like, pretty lady. Although I was thinking somewhere a little less crowded so we could get to know each other a little better."

Did this kind of thing really work on human women?

Something hit her sensitive ears. A growl. Distant. Quiet. But definitely there.

Curious, she leaned around the human and found the wolf watching their little exchange. His dance partner was watching them, too. Probably wondering who, or what, was taking his attention from her. She didn't look happy.

"What's your name, anyway?" the human asked her.

"Ryanne," she told him.

"That's a damn pretty name."

"Do you think so?" she said. She'd never really been a fan.

"So, what do you say, Ryanne?"

She gave his offer some serious consideration. The wolf would be here for a few hours, of that she was quite certain if his past behavior was any indication. It would give her plenty of time to go have a little carnal fun with the human and be back before he left. For she had no doubt that was exactly what this human had meant by "getting to know each other better".

And she sure could use a little fun.

Ryanne weighed the risks involved. She wasn't there to pick anyone up, but then again, if the offer was there, why not take it? And maybe she needed something to distract her from this shifter. Her interest in him was bordering on obsession and more importantly, it was veering her off course. She hadn't come to this part of the country to follow a werewolf around. No, she had much more important things to do. Another to find.

She smiled up at the human male, nodding along with her words to make sure he understood her over the music and shouted conversations. "Okay. Let's go."

The look of surprise on his face was almost comical, but he recovered quickly and pulled out his wallet. Tossing a few large bills on the bar— way more than the drinks could possibly cost, even with a tip - was it supposed to impress her? —he stuck out his elbow.

Ryanne hopped off her bar stool and took it. If he wanted to throw away his money, who was she to stop him? Besides, the humans behind the bar deserved it for putting up with some of the behavior in this club.

Forging a path through the throng of people vying for the space they'd just vacated at the bar, they were halfway to the front door when it was flung open and a group of three males came in.

Ryanne pulled her date to a halt, never taking her eyes from the newcomers. Something about them was setting off a red flag. They weren't acting like just a normal group of guys who were out for a night on the town.

She searched out the green-eyed shifter. He was leading his dance partner over to a table, one eye on the new guys even as he smiled and nodded in response to whatever the woman was saying. His jaw lifted and his nostrils flared, scenting the air. A second later, his entire body stiffened as his muscles visibly locked down.

Her instincts had been correct. These men were trouble.

She turned her attention back to the new group. They were spreading out, eyes scanning the club. She watched the way they moved, how carefully they placed their feet with each step, how alert they all were to every tiny sound, every movement of the people around them. The largest one stopped at the edge of the dance floor, his nose in the air.

Shifters. They were shifters. Predators seeking out prey. And by the way Green Eyes was watching them, they weren't local. Which meant they weren't of his pack.

This did not mean good things for her.

Ryanne's mind raced. There was a back door. By the bathrooms. Her date forgotten, she turned and started walking that way, keeping her steps slow and steady. It would do no good to run in an enclosed space like this. If she did, they would be upon her in a fraction of a heartbeat. And, somehow, she got the sense they wouldn't give two wits about the humans in their way.

She didn't know if they were there looking for her specifically, or if this was just some kind of messed up coincidence, but either way, if they found her here, her remaining time in this world would not be long.

And she wouldn't be the only casualty.

Out of the corner of her eye, she saw the green-eyed wolf heading in her direction and felt a flare of panic. Had she been wrong about him? Maybe he did know these shifters and she'd been a fool to think he didn't know who or what she was. Maybe he'd been planning this the entire time, and she'd played right into his hands by following him. By being so easy to find. Perhaps he'd just been stringing her along, waiting for her defenses to be down. Waiting for backup to be available because he knew she wouldn't be easy to catch.

Or easy to kill.

She'd been a stupid fool. And now, all would be lost.

The sound of breaking glass caught her attention. Ryanne whipped her head toward the sound just in time to see a human male, his face red with anger, hit another male in the jaw with his fist. What looked to be a beer bottle was smashed at his feet.

Before she could foresee what would happen, others jumped into the middle of the melee. Fists cracked into bone. Bodies were thrown into the crowd. Females screamed and covered their heads, trying to get out of the way.

And the path to the backdoor was effectively blocked.

Ryanne dodged a chair leg just before it hit her in the head and tried to find her own way through the tornado of flying fists and bar stools, each man intent on taking out his aggressions on another and not caring in the slightest who might be in his way. But it was no use, the entry to the hall was completely blocked.

Spinning around, she tried to see if she could sneak out the front. But keeping in the spirit of things, more fights had broken out, and there weren't enough bouncers in the world to stop this group once they'd gotten started. Unsurprisingly, her previous escort was right in the middle.

Ryanne took a calming breath. There was no way she could make it out unnoticed. Not without bringing attention to herself as being something "other". She started eyeing the vents high on the walls, wondering if she could possibly get into one without drawing notice.

Someone grabbed her around the upper arm, and Ryanne looked up into a pair of glowing green eyes.

"Come with me, lass. I can get ye tae safety."

Ryanne fought against his hold. "I'm perfectly capable of saving myself," she said. She didn't raise her voice, but she knew she didn't need to.

"I ken that. But ye dinna want tae bring attention tae yerself." He shoved off a man who stumbled into him in a distracted manner, throwing him back into the pile. Then he bent down to speak directly in her ear. "I dinna ken what those three want with ye, but ye'd been spotted right before th' fight broke out." He threw up an arm and easily blocked a punch that missed its intended victim and came straight toward them.

"Dammit," she said out loud.

"Aye," he agreed. "I swear I will no' harm ye, lass. But we

need tae go. And we need tae do it now." Without waiting for her to decide, he pulled her into his hard body, tucking her against his side.

One arm around her and one held straight out, he used it like a battering ram to force a path through the chaos. But to Ryanne's surprise, he didn't head toward either door. Instead, he made his way back to the bar. With a brief, apologetic smile, he crouched down and slipped an arm beneath her knees, lifting her up and over the counter and dropping her unceremoniously behind it. Then he placed one hand on the dented, wooden surface and hoisted himself up and over.

As soon as they were both behind the bar, he pulled her down out of sight. "We need tae get ye out o' this place." He scrubbed a hand over his mouth, and Ryanne found herself eyeing the masculine shadow of his beard. "Preferably without those shifters seeing us," he added.

"Why are you helping me?" she asked. Because she still wasn't certain this wasn't some sort of a trap.

Those glowing green eyes swung back to her. "Why have ye been following me?"

"I don't know," she told him honestly.

He gave her a small smile. "Aye. Me either."

A human landed on the floor beside them, writhing around in pain, one hand on his back, the heels of his boots trying to make purchase on the concrete floor.

Ryanne barely gave him a glance, preferring to study the shifter close up while she had the chance.

He was very good looking, this male. And he had a sexy

Scottish accent. Which perhaps explained his garbled greeting that first time he'd tried to talk to her. "Are you mated?" she asked with genuine curiosity. She couldn't see how he wouldn't be, but wondered why he would be here so often if had someone at home. From what she'd heard, shifters were notoriously loyal and possessive with their mates. Nearly as bad as the vampires.

That caught him by surprise. A red flush crept up his neck. "No, I'm no' mated. But maybe we can save this conversation for another time?"

She nodded. "Okay." Still, she had to wonder why some female hadn't latched onto this one a long time ago. Of course, if he had been mated, the fact that he came here multiple times a week to flirt with other women would have knocked him way down in her estimation of him.

He gave her a lopsided smile, a dimple appearing on one rugged cheek that seemed to have a direct link to the twinge of desire that suddenly had her clenching her thighs together. No wonder the human women practically fell over each other to dance with him if that was all it took to get a reaction out of her. She'd seen him turn on much more charm with the others and had to admit she was glad he was keeping things toned down with her. For if he didn't, she wasn't ashamed to admit she'd be nothing but a pile of raging hormones at his feet by now.

As people yelled and bodies slammed into tables and she waited to see what his plan to escape would be, her mind began to wander. Like why, after only trying to talk to her one time, he'd reverted back to only watching her from a distance? And why *didn't* he turn on the charm with her? Was she not attractive enough? The human males certainly seemed to think she was.

Her shifter peeked over the bar top and quickly crouched back down. "Tis only getting worse," he said. "We're just going tae have tae make a run for it."

She tried to focus on the problem at hand. "What about the others?"

His eyes flew back to hers, and Ryanne didn't see the answers she was hoping for. She tried again. "The other shifters? Who are they?"

"I dinna ken. But I dinna think we want them tae find ye."

She took a deep breath. Could she really trust him? What if he was only pretending to help her and took her right to them? Did she have a choice? "We could just stay here until things calm down."

But he was shaking his head before she'd even finished her sentence. "Then they will find ye for sure, lass. No. We have tae run, and we have tae do it now. While those wolves are tae busy tossin' humans tae notice."

He was right. Maybe she could let him get them to the back door, and then lose him as soon as she was out in the open and had a chance to run. Although if chafed her to let him take the lead, she could play the helpless female if it wouldn't draw undo attention to her. If she started muscling grown men out of her way or suddenly ran full speed through the fighting, she would surely lead the other shifters right to her.

Besides, this male was large enough that he could effectively hide her with his body. So, although the others had to know he was here—they would've scented him as he had them—they didn't seem overly concerned by his presence. And it would make him the perfect cover for her.

It also meant he had been right that they weren't there for him. They were there for her. "Dammit."

"Aye," he breathed. "Dinna fash yerself, lass. I'll make sure nothing happens tae ye." He paused. Took a breath. "Yer ready?"

She nodded.

"Front door or back?"

"Back."

"Aye. Agreed." He stood, looked around, and held out his hand.

Ryanne took it, and it was hard not to notice how her small hand was dwarfed in his large one. He had very nice hands with long fingers, and just rough enough not to feel feminine. She allowed him to pull her up to a standing position. But he didn't stop there.

Scooping her up into his powerful arms like she weighed no more than a bag of feathers, he tucked her in close to his body and headed over to the end of the bar. "Hang on, lass," he told her, and then he jumped up and over with her in his arms and pushed his way out into the throng of violence.

Keeping his head down, he held her close with one arm, hunching his shoulders and protecting her with his body, while he used the other arm to shove the brawling humans away as he fought his way toward the back door. Once they made it to the hallway where the bathrooms were, he could've put her down, but he didn't. Instead, he wrapped his other arm around her and pulled her in even closer to his chest. She felt the rise and fall of his breaths beneath her shoulder, calm and steady. And once, she thought she heard him say, "Och, sweet as a primrose." And then they were through the door and striding away from the club, his long legs eating up the pavement with each step.

No gang of werewolves was waiting outside to take her off his hands. Only the two police cars who had just pulled up, lights flashing and sirens blaring. Four officers jumped out and ran past them to the door they'd just come out of. Not one of them so much as spared them a glance.

Duncan's chest rumbled against her body as he gave them a warning growl. Just in case.

Ryanne found his protectiveness amusing and...kind of nice. But enough was enough. "You can put me down now, shifter."

He threw a surprised glance her way, but he didn't stop to do as she asked. "Ye ken what I am, lass?"

"Aye," she told him with a smirk. "Possibly from the sheer volume of the growls I heard coming from your direction when the other shifters came in. Or perhaps it's the way those green eyes of your glow, like one of those strange fish who live at the bottom of the ocean." She looked at him thoughtfully. "Actually, I knew it the first time I saw you."

He checked over his shoulder before glancing down at her again. It was only a brief look before he went back to scanning the area around them, but she didn't miss the expression of caution that came over his features or the way her heart sped up by the close proximity of his mouth to hers. "Aye. In th' forest."

"Yes."

"And what were ye doing there? Yer a Faerie, are ye no'?"

"So, you know what I am, too."

They reached his Jeep and he finally set her down. As though he loathed to let her go, his hands lingered a moment too long before they slowly slid away and he straightened. His eyes wandered down to her booted feet and back again. He swallowed hard. "I knew it the first time I saw ye," he mimicked.

Ryanne's pulse was pounding, and it had nothing to do with the close call she'd just had and everything to do with the way this wolf was looking at her. "Well, thank you for getting me out of the club."

He gave her a nod. "Twas my honor tae help ye, lass."

To her surprise, Ryanne found herself disinclined to leave him just yet, but she needed to be far away from this place when those other shifters figured out they'd left. "We should talk more. Another time."

"Aye," he breathed. His eyes travelled over her face. "Uh…I dinna think ye should hang around here. Can I give ye a ride…anywhere?"

Ryanne wondered what it was about her person that caused him to act so unlike himself. As she was short on time, she cut right to the chase. "Why don't you flirt with me?"

His eyes widened and he brought his fist up to his

mouth, coughing self-consciously. He opened his mouth to say something…

Ryanne watched as his big body suddenly stilled. Everything about him became suddenly…aware, though his eyes never moved from her face. "What's wrong?"

"Get in th' Jeep, lass." Though the words were nothing more than a deep rumble, the underlying tone beneath them had her searching the area around them. She saw nothing. Heard nothing.

The shifter grabbed her wrist. "Ye need tae get in th' Jeep, and ye need tae do it NOW. Please," he added.

She wouldn't normally hop into a vehicle with a stranger, and especially not with a shifter, but there was no mistaking the urgency in his tone. And he hadn't caused her any harm. Actually, he'd done the exact opposite.

He didn't take her to the passenger side, but pulled her past him, blocking her with his body as he directed her into the driver's side. Sniffing the air, he scanned the area around the club as he opened the door. "Hurry, lass. They're coming."

She got in and crawled over to the passenger side.

He got in right behind her. Locking the door, he started the Jeep.

"Who are those males?" she asked.

"I dinna ken, but they are no' from around here." Throwing the Jeep into gear, he checked the rearview mirror and backed out of his spot. "And they're coming for ye."

Ryanne looked out the back windshield just as the three

shifter males came around the corner of the club. They spotted them pulling out immediately and with nothing but a look exchanged between them, they started jogging after the Jeep.

"Fookin' hell," her driver muttered. He upshifted into third gear, swerving into the oncoming lane to get around the slower traffic while he dug a phone out of his front pocket. Holding it up in front of his face, he tapped the screen and held it to his ear. "Cedric, it's me. I'm in Seattle, and makin' a quick getaway. Three wolves came walkin' in tae th' club tonight." He paused. "No, this in no' a bad joke. I'm being serious." Another pause. "I dinna ken who they are or where they came from." Glancing at Ryanne, he said. "I have a lass with me, a—"

Grabbing his arm, Ryanne shook her head.

He frowned at her. "—a...a...I mean, I would've gotten out sooner but I had tae help a lass get out o' the bar. No. I dinna ken. Och, aye. I'll text ye when I get home." Weaving in and out of traffic with one hand, he checked the rearview again. "No. I got out quick. I dinna want tae lead them tae our home. Aye. I will." He hung up the phone, shoving it back into his pocket.

Silence filled the vehicle. He didn't ask her why she didn't want his friend to know about her, and that surprised her. "Thank you," she finally told him. "For not saying anything about my being here. I'm trying to stay off the radar."

"Aye," he said. "I'm sorry. I was no' thinkin'. Are they still followin' us?"

She twisted around in her seat. "Yes."

One side of his mouth curved into that lopsided smile that jarred all the things inside of her. When he looked at her, excitement danced in his green eyes. "Then ye better buckle up, lass."

CHAPTER 3

D uncan tried to slow his racing heart, but it was impossible to do with his mysterious lass sitting right beside him.

Right there beside him.

In his Jeep.

Blethering on with him about the wolves who had come into the club and ruined his night.

Not that it hadn't already been ruined by the fact that his mysterious stalker had been about to leave with someone else. A human, for Christ's sake. And one wearing one of those stupid hats.

However, whoever had started the brawl? Aye, he'd be thanking him the next time he saw him. Buy the man a beer. Because of him and his temper, Duncan had had the perfect opportunity to hold the lass in his arms. To feel her soft curves and smell her sweet scent.

It was as though fate had intervened to put the two of

them together. Aye, it was fate, and had nothing at all to do with the fact that he'd barreled through fists flying at his face and leapt over tables to get to her. Luckily, everyone had been too busy either fightin' or fleein' to pay much attention.

A quick look in the rearview mirror confirmed the lass was right. Those three wolves were running full out behind them now, not caring at all who might see them. Duncan growled low in his throat and she looked over at him, one eyebrow lifted in question. Gods, but she was bonnie. A braw female, for sure.

And she was a Faerie. Of the *na maithe* tribe, if he were to take a guess. Because if she were anything else…

No. He wouldn't even think of it.

He'd figured it out the first time he'd seen her when she'd run off with the speed of a vamp. If it wasn't for the fact that it was day at the time, he couldn't have been convinced she wasn't one. However, vampires would never be running about in the woods in the middle of the day. Even with the canopy of the trees, it was too risky. They could be exposed to the sun, and anything more than a few seconds and they'd be a cloud of ash blowing through the pines.

And he'd known she wasn't a shifter. He would've scented another of his kind a mile away out in the open like that. So, that left only one other thing he knew of that she could be.

And tonight, when he had her wee self in his arms, he'd caught a good whiff of her. She didn't smell like a wolf, or a vamp. She smelled like primrose, blooms from his homeland.

And he would bet she tasted just as sweet.

Another growl rose in his throat, this one hungry with lust. To feel this way again shook him through and through, and he cleared his throat, trying to disguise the sound before the lass heard.

"They're getting closer," she said.

Duncan closed his eyes for a second, letting the sweet tones of her voice rain over him. "We're almost tae th' freeway. They will no' be able tae keep up with us then."

"Are you sure about that?"

Steel infused his back and he gripped the steering wheel as he told her, "Aye, lass. I will no' let them get tae ye. Dinna fash yerself."

"How are you so certain they're after me?"

At the last minute, Duncan spun the wheel, heading east instead of north. He'd lead them out to the mountains. If this came down to a fight, it would be better to be away from his home and out of sight of the humans, and there would be less traffic this way. "I saw th' way th' leader latched on to ye at th' club. They had no interest in me at all, and they knew I was there."

"Are you sure about that?"

"Aye, lass. I can smell another wolf th' second he or she comes into th' room. Miles away sometimes if we're out in th' open. It would be th' same for any shifter."

"Really? That far?"

"Aye." Duncan checked the mirrors and merged onto the

highway. Making his way to the far-left lane, he stomped on the gas.

"What's your name, wolf?"

He opened his mouth to tell her, paused, and only said, "Duncan. My name is Duncan. What's yours?"

She repeated his name, then told him hers. "Ryanne."

He felt her eyes on him. Watching him for a reaction. "Ryanne," he repeated. "That's a bonnie name. It suits ye."

He felt her visibly relax beside him. It was obvious she didn't want him to know a lot about her. But if she was there on some kind of secret mission, why follow him around? Why expose her presence when she did?

"They shifted," she told him. "They're coming," she added a little louder. "Duncan." Facing front, she tightened her seat belt.

"Aye, I see them." He stomped down on the clutch and shifted into fifth gear, hitting the gas hard. The fookers were fast, but he knew these roads. Knew these woods. And he was faster. He had to be. There was no way he was going to let them get their paws on Ryanne. He didn't know why they were after her, but he assumed it was because she was Fae. Even though the war was over, there was still a lot of packs who hunted them.

He, himself, was still somewhat wary of the forest people. Although a few of his friends and pack mates had mated with Fae lasses, and Duncan tried not to treat them any differently than any other, if he were to be honest with himself, they still struck fear in his bones.

Even the sweet thing sitting beside him.

But that hadn't stopped his wolf from rushing to her side when danger arose. And once his beast had made it's mind up about something, there was no stopping it.

Even if it meant taking on the three who were following them.

It was a perplexing thing, that the beast inside of him was so adamant about this particular lass, and it was definitely something to think about when he had a moment's peace. However, Duncan quickly shoved the thought aside. He had no time to worry about it at the moment. Right now, he just needed to get her to safety, and then get back to his pack and tell them what he knew about these wolves who were invading Cedric's territory without the alpha's permission.

"I think we're losing them," Ryanne said. The relief she felt was evident in her tone.

Duncan checked the mirror. Then he checked again. He looked to either side of the vehicle, then behind them again.

"What's wrong?"

"There's only two wolves back there," he told her. "I dinna ken where th' third one is." Duncan floored the gas pedal. The police could just add to the chase if they happened to see him.

Ryanne held one hand up the window, shielding her eyes from any glare from the lights on the dashboard, though he knew she could see as well as he could in the darkness. Twisting around, she searched behind them, then leaned across his lap to look out his window, the dark curls pulled on top of her head softly brushing his jaw.

He inhaled the sweet smell of her.

Fookin' hell.

His insides twisted, and for a few seconds, he completely forgot where he was and what he was supposed to be doing. But then she was gone again, back on her own side of the Jeep.

His wolf howled at the loss, pacing restlessly beneath his skin. Duncan took a deep breath and focused on the dark road ahead of him.

"Where did it go?" she asked him.

"I dinna ken. But this can no' be good."

"You have to lose them. If they catch me…" She let the words trail away.

He knew well what would happen if they caught her. The Fae weren't ones he would ever mess with if there was no need. At least not one on one. But there were three of those wolves. If he thought he could take them alone, he'd stop the Jeep and shift, but one against three weren't very good odds. If he took on one, or even two, that would leave the last one to go after Ryanne. And it was very possible, in all the confusion of a fight, it would get its jaws around her wee throat before she could protect herself. "I'm tryin', lass." He glanced over.

She was looking at him with large dark eyes. Eyes full of worry and something else.

Trust.

"They will no' get their paws on ye," he promised her. Motioning with his head, he indicated the "oh, shit!" handles beside her seat and along the top of her window. "Hang on, Ryanne. We're aboot tae go off road."

Checking behind them, he saw he was finally gaining ground, although there was still no sign of the third wolf. Of course, it didn't mean anything. It could've broken off from the others in an attempt to cut them off further ahead.

Or maybe he'd gotten taken out by one of the big trucks, the only other vehicles on this dark highway this late at night. It wasn't likely, but one could hope.

Perhaps if they fought together...

No, he couldn't risk it.

He wouldn't take the chance of getting hurt, or even killed, and leaving his female defenseless.

Duncan frowned. Where the fook had that come from? The lass wasn't his.

Did he want her to be?

Och. Now was not the time to be thinking about such a matter. Their only chance was to get out of their sight and lose them, then circle back and get to his pack.

He watched the landscape as they sped down the highway. The turn he was looking for would be coming up very soon. If he could get around it, their pursuers would lose sight of them, and there was a turnoff on the left. An old, dirt road that led up the mountain, completely unnoticeable if you didn't know it was there, half covered with overhanging branches and brush covering the tire tracks. The highway began to weave in and out through the mountains here. With any luck, they could disappear into the trees and be gone by the time the wolves chasing them came around the corner.

"Hang on," he told his passenger. "The turn off is just ahead."

Ryanne gripped the handles, leaning her body forward. "I don't see anything."

"Oh, it's there," he told her. "Just a little ways more…" He checked the mirror as they started around the curve. The wolves disappeared from his line of his sight just as he'd hoped. Cutting off the headlights, he wrenched the steering wheel to the left, cut across the grassy median—just missing an oncoming truck—and drove straight into the trees.

Downshifting into low gear, Duncan crawled up the side of the mountain, praying to all the gods the big engine of that truck would hide the noise of the Jeep. He didn't worry about them seeing him. His Vina was painted the perfect color green to blend in with the forest around them, just like the lady she was named after.

Ryanne laughed as they bumped along up the mountain, soft, throaty notes that were music to his ears, and despite the danger they were in, he couldn't help a small smile in return.

About a mile or so up, he pulled off the trail, wedging the Jeep between some thick pine trees, and cut the engine.

"What are we doing?" Ryanne asked.

"We're waiting," he told her. "If I keep going, there's a verra good chance they'll double back and hear us. So, we'll sit. And we'll wait. And stay inside where they will no' scent either o' us."

"For how long?" She sounded almost disappointed that the excitement was over.

"As long as it takes, lass. Sometimes, although it may no' be as exciting, patience is th' best practice."

She didn't look convinced, but she didn't argue anymore. Sighing loudly, she stared out the front windshield. Duncan did the same, cracking his window a bit, but there was no sign of the strange wolves by sight, sound, or scent. Only the pungent aroma of the pine trees, wet from the misty rain.

Now that they were out of danger, at least for the moment, Duncan found he could think of nothing at all to say. His usual sugary tongue felt like it was coated in tar, heavy with bland and boring words, just like the one other time he'd tried to speak to her. It was a predicament, and he didn't know what to do about it. Talking to females was not a problem he'd ever had before. So much so, he was often accused of being a flirt.

And maybe he was. Though most of the time, he did it on purpose just to rile up their males. And other times, he did it just to prove that he could...

He gave himself a mental shake. What had he been thinking about?

Oh, aye. The lass beside him. She was a mystery. But more than that, there was something unique about her. He found himself craving her company at odd moments, and yet he could barely utter a word when he was finally near her. He felt like a right *eejit*, hoping every day to see her, and then not knowing how to act when he did.

"So, what pack are you from?" she asked, pulling him from his contemplations.

Her question surprised him. "Ye dinna ken?" When she shook her head, he told her, "I'm part o' th' Pacific Northwest pack." He paused, but only briefly, because for some reason he could only say nothing at all or blather on like he didn't have an ounce of sense in his head when he was around her. "I live here. I'm supposed tae be here. I'm no'…" he stumbled to a halt. Och. Why could he not seem to form a coherent thought? It was better when the wolves were chasing them. At least then, his own wolfish instincts had taken over and kept him focused.

For the most part.

"Does it hurt?"

He frowned, wondering if she could read his thoughts. Aye, it did hurt. Verra bad. He was not the stumbling fool she must think him to be. And honestly, he didn't know if his ego could take the beating.

"When you shift. Does it hurt?"

Oh. That. "Aye, it hurts."

"Can you stop it?"

"Stop it from hurting?"

"No. Stop the shift. Can you stop it from happening?"

Duncan didn't see the harm in telling her. "Sometimes. Sometimes no'."

"Like when you're angry?"

"Aye, if my temper gets th' best o' me."

"Can you shift at will? Or do you have to be mad or something?"

He tried to guess the reasoning behind her questions. "If yer worried whether I can take care o' ye if those other shifters show up, dinna fash yerself. Me and my wolf will do what needs tae be done, and all ye will need tae do is run th' way I seen ye do before."

Something hit the windshield, and she jumped.

"It's just a pinecone, lass. Knocked down by the rain."

She watched drops hit the windshield, nodding. But he could hear her heart pounding and her breath whooshing in and out of her lungs at a rapid rate. Tentatively, he reached over and placed his hand over hers, still tight on the hand grip. "Ryanne, I swear tae ye, I will no' let them harm ye. I will protect ye with my life if th' need arises."

Her head tilted, little lines furrowing the smooth skin between her eyebrows. "Why would you do that?"

Why, indeed? He didn't know, but he felt it with certainty all the way down to his bones. "Yer..." He started to say something along the lines of her being a female, and therefore needing his protection. But then he stopped. That wasn't right. She didn't need his protection. He knew first-hand what a Fae lass was capable of. Although three wolves at once would be a bit much, she could easily outrun them if she had a head start.

Duncan thought about that for a minute.

Heat crept up his neck to burn his cheeks. Had she been playing with him? Allowing him to play the big, strong male and lead her to safety? "I dinna ken," he ground out. "Ye obviously dinna need my help."

She gave him a funny look. "No, I probably didn't. But it was nice to have it anyway."

If his face burned before, now it was so hot he raised a hand to touch the skin of his cheek, just to check if it was melting from the bone. He'd acted a fool. Involving himself in something he shouldn't have, when what he should've been doing was hightailing it out of the club and reporting back to Cedric.

Conflict rumbled deep in his chest, and he rubbed the center of it. But what if something had happened to the lass? What if she wasn't able to get around the humans? What if she'd been seen as the supernatural she is? Or worse, what if the wolves had caught her before she got out? She could be lying in a ditch on the side of the road, the life seeping out of her...

Och. He was turning into his maw!

The gods rest her soul.

"Duncan."

He pulled himself from his thoughts. It was hard to look at her, feeling foolish as he was, but somehow, he managed. "Aye?"

The smile that lit her face was tiny and sweet and stopped his heart completely. "Thank you. For helping me get out of the club and to safety."

Words tumbled around on his tongue, but his throat closed and he was unable to utter any of them. So, instead, he just nodded.

"Do you scent those wolves? Are they anywhere near us?"

He turned his nose to the window and breathed deep. Turning back to her, he shook his head.

She unbuckled her seat belt. Leaning toward him, she caught his eyes. "It's very, very important you tell no one about me. No one," she emphasized. "Not even your alpha. Okay?"

Overcome by the sight and scent and warmth of her so close to him, Duncan nodded. "Aye, lass. No one will know ye were here."

"Thank you," she whispered. Then she pressed a kiss to his still-burning cheek. Before he could regain the ability to do more than blink at her, she opened the door and hopped out into the rain.

Duncan jumped out his side and ran around the front of the Jeep. To do what? Say something to make her stay? To see if he would ever see her again? But she had left him as she had before, running away into the forest faster than his eye could track her. The rain that kept them hidden from the wolves also washing away her scent.

Arrows tore through his chest, until he was near doubled over from the loss.

CHAPTER 4

Marc walked into the apartment he shared with Bronaugh. Since moving in with him, she hadn't been shy about making the place her own. Tapestries hung behind the couch and covered the walls of their bedroom. Giant scenes of trees and birds and landscapes.

Setting down the bag of groceries, he scented the air. The smell of meadowsweet flowers tickled his nose and his body instantly hardened, sensing his mate was near. "Bronaugh, lass? Where are ye?"

The kitchen and living room were empty, as was the guest bathroom. He left the groceries on the counter and went to the bedroom, his instincts now on high alert.

Something was wrong.

As he passed through the living room, he flicked a glance at a new hanging on the wall—a black raven surrounded by storm clouds. His steps paused for just a moment. The art piece was dark, too dark for his liking.

An uneasy feeling slithered up his spine.

Walking into the bedroom, his eyes flew around the room, searching for the bright hair of his mate. The door to the bathroom was only partially closed, and he called her name again as he approached, not wanting to catch her doing anything she would be embarrassed about. Not that his lass was shy about much.

She wasn't in there, either.

Now truly worried, he glanced around again. Perhaps she was out on the balcony? But, no. No. He could smell her sweet scent. She was near. "Bronaugh, lass. Ye ken all I have tae do is shift and I will find ye. So, ye may as well save me th' trouble."

His Bronaugh was *an olc*. As one of the dark magic Faeries, she could hide in plain sight from humans and shifters alike. But she couldn't hide from his wolf. Och. No. His wolf could find her every time.

He snapped his head around at a slight shift of movement behind him. His lass stood behind him near the bathroom, blond hair in disarray, wearing only one of his T-shirts. It fell nearly to her knees.

But the untidiness of her appearance wasn't what had him taking an unconscious step toward her. It was the meekness of her pose and the unusual colors radiating from her normally brown eyes. Reds and oranges dominated, like a rainbow from hell mystically caught within the orbs. "Bronaugh, lass, what's wrong? Why are ye hiding from me?"

"I wasn't hiding," she told him. "I was just…hiding."

"Aye, I can see that. What is th' reason? Did something happen? Are ye hurt? Did someone say something tae ye?" He was in front of her before he realized he'd told his feet to move—his upper lip curled back, his canines aching to bite into whoever had dared to cause any sort of upset to his mate.

But she stepped back, putting distance between them again. "No. No. I'm fine. No one has been here."

"Yer no' fine," he nearly shouted. Taking a deep breath, he tempered his tone. "Yer no' fine, lass. Please tell me wha' is going on with ye. Before I go mad."

A smile teased the corners of her sweet mouth. "You wolves are so damn emotional."

"Aye," he confirmed as his skin shifted over the muscle on his back and shoulders. "And mine are on th' verge o' burstin' free tae save my mate from whatever is hurting her, so ye better start speaking." He paused, giving her a chance to answer him. When she didn't, but only continued to look at him with those haunted eyes, the pain nearly brought him to his knees. His lass was suffering. And it nearly killed him to be unable to take it from her. "Bronaugh, *please* tell me. I canna stand it."

She looked toward the window and ran a hand through her hair, and now he could see why it was sticking out all over her head. "I think I just need to go."

"Go?" he asked. "Go where? It's no' th' best time, but Cedric will understand if I have tae leave…"

"No," she said. "I meant by myself. I need to go alone."

Marc stilled. He didn't like where this conversation was

heading. Not at all. Closing the distance between them, he cupped her wee face in his hand.

But she backed away again, and when she looked at him, her beautiful eyes were bright with unshed tears. "No, Marc. You need to stay away from me. I couldn't live with myself if I hurt you."

He started to go to her, but she held up her hand, halting him in his tracks. Her anxiety was plain to see in the way she held her shoulders and fisted her hands at her sides. "Damn it all, lass. I can no' just stand here and do nothing! And I can no' let ye leave me." His voice broke on the last. "That is no' happening, do ye hear me? So, we will talk this out. Whatever it is. And we will figure out how tae fix it."

"There is no 'fixing it', Marc."

The lack of hope in her voice and posture scared him more than if she were lunging for his throat. "Dinna say that, Bronaugh. Tis no' true."

"It is," she whispered.

No. No. He would not believe it. "Maybe if ye tell me what's happening…give me a chance tae…"

"It's the darkness, Marc. It's taking over."

His breath stopped, and it took a concentrated effort to get his lungs working again. "No, Bronaugh." And then he said it again, stronger this time, as though he could stop what was happening by his will alone. "NO, Bronaugh."

The sorrow in her eyes as she watched him struggle was more than he could stand. He turned away. Paced to the window and back. This could not be happening. He would not let it happen.

"I knew it was a risk when I allowed that part of me to come forth down in Texas. But I had to do it. I had to do it to save you, Marc." She was pleading with him now. For what? For him to understand?

A growl rumbled deep in his throat. Though he'd tried to erect a wall around them, memories broke through. Things he'd never wanted to think of again. Memories of his Bronaugh with two broken legs sitting atop the black wolf at the fookin' rodeo that Texas alpha had thought would be good entertainment for his pack. His Bronaugh had saved him that day. And the black wolf was dead.

And by an act of the gods, Keegan had fallen for one of the "stars" of his show. Now the rodeo was no more, but the trauma it had caused was still alive and well.

She had saved his life that day. And now, he would save hers.

"Tell me wha' ye need, Bronaugh, and I will make it happen."

"I need to go away, before I hurt someone here. Before I hurt you." She paused, her mouth twisting into something that had no resemblance to a smile. "I feel it rising within me every day, Marc. The anger. The need to cause pain. And more than that. The hunger…"

"Nothing can hurt me more than yer leaving me would."

"You're wrong."

"I'm no' wrong!" he shouted. "Fook!" Closing his eyes, he pressed his palms into his pounding temples and took a moment. He wasn't angry at her. Gods, no. He was angry at himself for ignoring what had been happening right in front of his own fookin' eyes all this time. For not trying harder to stop her from calling on the evil within her that first time.

For not saving her from herself.

The warmth of her fingers penetrated through his shirt. They slid briefly down his chest, and he dropped his arms. That simple touch was enough to calm the beast inside of him, and he immediately wanted more. Selfish bastard that he was.

Grasping her hand between both of his, he hung on and wouldn't let go. Even when she tried to pull away. "No, Bronaugh. I'm no' letting ye go." He had to force the words out from between clenched teeth.

"You have to, Marc. I'm losing control. I'll hurt you."

"Then do it, lass. Hurt me if that's what ye need."

She stared at him like he'd lost his mind. And perhaps he had. But life without his Bronaugh would be no life at all.

"You don't know what you're saying."

"I do. I ken exactly what I'm saying. Do what ye need tae do tae ease th' beast inside o' ye, lass. I understand that need, more than ye ken. Ye will no' hurt me. And even if ye do, I'm a shifter. A werewolf. I'll heal."

She shook her head, even as a glimmer of hope sparked in her colorful eyes. "Marc…"

He bared his teeth at her. "Do. It. Bronaugh."

Tears overflowed onto her cheeks, and his wolf howled at the proof of her pain. Still shaking her head, she tried to pull away. "I just need to go."

"No." The word came out more as a growl than anything.

And then he was pulling her into his arms and slamming his mouth to hers, needing to feel her soft body against him. Needing to feed the connection between them.

She resisted, pressing her lips together. Not letting him in.

Marc nipped at her bottom lip. Hard. Drawing blood. Desperate. Near crazed with the need to keep her with him.

Bronaugh moaned deep in her throat and gripped his hips, her nails digging through his jeans. Her lips parted, her tongue teasing his.

"Aye, lass," he whispered against her mouth. "Dinna be afraid. I want this. I want ye."

A growl that would rival any of his rose within her. She bit at his jaw, his throat. Her hands were under his shirt now, ripping the buttons from the flannel to have better access to his skin.

Marc groaned as her sharp, little teeth sank into the muscle of his pec. With a shove from his wee lass, he was spun around and slammed against the wall where she had been just a moment before. His shirt was ripped from his shoulders, then his jeans were undone, his stiff cock freed and her wee hand wrapped around him.

He kicked off his boots as she tore off the shirt she wore. Lifting her off her feet, he took them to the bed, her legs wrapping around his waist like she was born to be there. She ground her core against him, slick and hot, and Marc's knees nearly gave out at the feel of her. But he wouldn't disrespect her by taking her on the floor.

His Bronaugh was like a wild thing in his arms, and he

barely made it to the bed before she was rolling him over. Shoving his jeans down to his thighs, she took him in her hand and sank onto him, until he was buried to his balls inside of her. Immediately, she began to move, rocking her hips, fucking him hard.

Their mating was desperate and violent, and Marc ground his jaw together, his wolf clawing near the surface.

With an evil smile, Bronaugh leaned over him, grabbing his hands and holding them down on either side of his head. She took the muscle between his neck and shoulder between her teeth, and with a low growl, she bit down, holding him helpless beneath her as she had her way with him.

He yelled out her name as he came inside of her. Hard. Violent.

But she wasn't finished with him, yet.

An hour later, Marc sat naked on the floor and cradled her in his lap as she cried. He had bite marks all over him, a few other wounds that were still bleeding, and he thought he'd heard a bone crack in one of forearms the third time around. He glanced around the room. The bed was torn apart, but the rest of the room had survived with a minimum of damage.

However, none of that mattered one wit to him. The only thing he cared about was that the angry reds and oranges had faded from his Bronaugh's eyes, eventually replaced by the pinks, greens, blues, and yellows he knew. And now they were, once again, the deep, warm brown he associated with her when he had loved her well. He ran the fingers of his good hand through her blonde locks. "Shhhh, Bronaugh lass. It's alright. Ye dinna do anything tae me that won't be healed in another hour or so."

"I'm so sorry," she cried into his chest.

"I'm no' sorry at all," he told her. "How do ye feel?"

"I feel horrible," she admitted. Her eyes found his face, and she touched his cheek. "I can't believe you let me do that."

"I can handle yer passion, lass."

"That was more than just passion."

"Aye, and I can handle that, tae. Whatever ye need, Bronaugh, I'm here for ye. Just dinna talk aboot leaving me. No' ever again." He tried his injured arm, and found he was able to move it. The bone was nearly knitted back together. Taking her face between his hands, he forced her to look at him. "I love ye, lass. More than my own life. And I will no' be losing ye tae yer dark side. Do ye hear me? I will no'. If ye need someone tae take it out on, ye come find me. Anytime, day or night." He smiled, trying to lighten the weight on her shoulders. "Wha' male would no' love his lass tae be so unable tae resist him she had tae sink her teeth into him?"

She laughed, and the light came back into his life. Leaning into him, she kissed him hard on the mouth. "I love you, Marc."

"I love ye, my Bronaugh. More than my own life." Wrapping her in his arms again, he released a breath he hadn't realized he'd been holding and tucked her head back against his chest so she couldn't see the worry in his eyes. "It will be alright, Bronaugh, lass. I swear it tae ye. Dinna fash yerself."

CHAPTER 5

Ryanne shivered in the drizzly rain that managed to find a way through the thick canopy above her. It would've been much more comfortable to stay in the dry warmth of the Duncan's Jeep, but she didn't trust herself to stay there. Listening to him, being so close to him, she'd started to...feel things. Things she had no business feeling. That shifter was too distracting, and her obsession with him needed to stop.

She gave a derisive laugh as the cabin she'd been staying in came into view. It wasn't hers. It belonged to the wolves. She'd found it weeks ago when she'd first seen Duncan and his friend in the forest. They'd been spying on Keelin's house, and Ryanne had been doing the same. All of them watching Duana, the *an olc* princess, search the house with her soul suckers.

Ryanne had come there to talk to Keelin, and her heart had stopped when she saw the princess had beat her there.

Keelin was The Key. Keelin had to be protected. And she had no idea where she was now.

When she'd found the two shifters spying from the trees, it had taken Ryanne off guard. Not knowing what else to do, she'd run. But not before she'd caught the eyes of the one closest to her. Bright green eyes that had flashed with danger when he'd spotted her, only to settle into something else entirely. Something she couldn't read.

And when she'd come across the cabin later that day, she knew it must belong to the wolves. It smelled like them, masculine and earthy, although the place felt cold and empty, like no one had been there for a while. Taking to the trees, she'd watched for them to return. And when, a few hours after nightfall, they hadn't returned, Ryanne jumped down and went inside. It was the perfect little shelter for her while she tried to find out what happened to Keelin.

Ryanne opened the door and went inside, immediately shucking off her wet clothing and leaving them in a pile on the floor where they landed. Barefoot and naked, she loaded the small stove with wood and got a small fire going, letting the heat dry her. She had a wistful thought of the days when her people could run around naked as wood nymphs all the time, before the humans came in such droves with their strange beliefs that the nude form was something bad. Something to be ashamed of.

Pfft.

Her body was strong and sensual and capable of feeling love and loss and pain and hope. It was not something she was ashamed of, nor would it ever be.

Something scratched at the door. Expecting her late-night visitor, she hadn't shut it tight, and sure enough, it was pushed open just wide enough to allow a fat, furry burglar inside. He stopped when he saw her standing there, his eyes wide and unblinking behind his mask until he realized who she was. Then he waddled over to the fire and sat beside her foot.

The little raccoon had also been staying at the cabin. Probably longer than Ryanne had. She brought him treats and shared the heat, and he allowed her to stay.

"Hello," she told him with a smile.

He didn't answer, sitting back on his haunches and holding his little hands out like he was warming them.

Ryanne walked over to the small kitchen and pulled out the bag of peanuts she'd found there the first night and brought them back over to the stove. She pulled one out and handed it to the raccoon, watching him with a smile as he deftly pulled it out of its shell and nibbled on it. She pulled one out for herself, tucked the bag under her arm to free her hands, and did the same.

She was glad he'd come back. She liked the company. It had been a long time since she'd had a friend.

As she shared her dinner of nuts, Ryanne used the peaceful lull of the early morning hours to revisit the reason she had travelled so far to come to this place. She had to face the truth. She was being way too careless. If she didn't get a grip on herself, she would be discovered. And she wasn't ready for anyone to know, yet. Allowing the shifter to see her was bad enough. Letting him get to know her was much too dangerous.

A stab of sorrow went through her when she thought of never seeing him again. But it had to be done. The chances that he knew the one she was seeking out here were slim, but one could never be too careful when it came to revenge on one's father.

With a sigh, she set three more peanuts on the floor beside her new friend and put the rest back in the cabinet. Then she put some more wood on the fire and went over to the small bed. When the sun came up, she was going to make her way down to Keelin's house and see if she could find anything that would give her a clue as to where she was, because it was now very apparent she wasn't coming back.

Crawling beneath the sleeping bags, she said goodnight to the little bandit and tried to get some sleep.

In the darkness, bright, green eyes found her, and a Scottish brogue swore she would not be getting away so easily.

Ryanne breathed in his masculine, earthy scent and smiled in her sleep.

CHAPTER 6

W hen Duncan got home, he went straight to his apartment and got in the shower. Then he put a load of laundry in the washer, including the clothes he'd been wearing, and texted Cedric to let him know he was back and would come see him first thing after they'd both gotten some sleep. He had promised Ryanne he would tell no one about her, and he was taking no chances that any of his brothers got a whiff of a strange Fae lass on him or his clothing. They would never believe him if he told them he'd only danced with her at the club.

He glanced around his room, double checking he hadn't forgotten anything. Then he crawled naked into bed to try to get some rest.

The sun had been up a good three hours when it finally roused him. He woke up in an unexplainable panic, heart pounding near out of his chest. Grabbing his phone from the nightstand, he checked for missed calls or messages. But there was nothing. No one was looking for him. He hadn't been missed, nor was he forgetting about something he was supposed to do.

Sitting up, he ran his hands through his hair and over his face. It must have been a dream.

He texted Cedric to see where he was, and when he received confirmation that he was at home, Duncan showered once more for good measure and brushed his teeth twice. He wasn't sure why. He hadn't kissed the lass or anything. Yet somehow, he still had the taste of her in his mouth.

Ten minutes later, he was knocking on his alpha's door. He was right glad they lived in the same building. For the sun that had so cheerfully woken him up had only been making a quick guest appearance and was now hidden behind some angry looking clouds. The threat of a good rain hung heavy in the air.

Hearing voices within the apartment, Duncan let himself inside. Cedric was standing by the window, speaking quietly with Marc. When he saw Duncan, he slapped Marc on the shoulder. "Dinna fash yerself. Just keep an eye on her and tell me if anything more happens."

"Aye," Marc told him. He gave Duncan a tight smile, slapping him on the back of the arm as he passed before he let himself out of the apartment.

There could only be one "her" they'd been speaking of— Marc's mate—and Duncan felt a keen sense of unease roll through him. Bronaugh was one of the *an olc*—the Dark Fae —though she'd been raised by two *na maithe* parents, the ones who didn't turn into zombie-like corpses running around trying to suck out souls because they didn't have any.

Some said it was an addiction, like the humans with their heroin and such, but Duncan didn't know if he believed that. He thought they were more like vampires. Feeding on those who had what they craved.

And if the problem Bronaugh was having was what caused that expression on Marc's face, Duncan was right worried about his brother. The words he'd spoken to Cedric just the day before ringing in his ears.

"Good Mornin', Duncan."

"Mornin', Cedric."

"How was yer night off?"

He pulled himself from his thoughts with effort. "Sorry, wha'?"

"I asked ye how yer night off was. Or did I dream that phone call last night?"

Right. The wolves. "It was interesting. As I told ye, I went into th' city and ran into some wolves there that were no' from around here. But they came walkin' in like they belonged, sure enough, their balls practically dragging th' ground."

Cedric's ears perked up at that last bit. "Ye dinna say? Wha' pack do they belong tae?"

"I dinna ken."

"Well, ye look like ye made it away without a scratch."

"Aye." He paused, thinking carefully what words to say that wouldn't give away his Ryanne. "I got th' feeling it was no' me they were looking for. They barely gave me a glance, though they had tae ken I was there. I smelled them th' moment they walked in, and they would've done th' same."

"Who were they looking for then?"

"I dinna ken." And that was the truth. He didn't. Not for certain. Though one could argue that they wouldn't have been chasing his Jeep if it hadn't been for the passenger he'd had with him. But he did not know that for sure. He hadn't heard any of them threaten her or call her name. Perhaps it had been a case of mistaken identity? "A fight broke out in th' club where I was—humans, no' wolves—and I went out th' back door and hightailed it back home." Also true. For the most part.

Cedric frowned, his eerie eyes sharp as they studied Duncan's face. But he was confident his alpha would find nothing to make him think Duncan hadn't been telling the truth. Nor would he scent a lie. For he'd told him everything as it had happened. Perhaps not the whole truth, but the truth, nonetheless.

"Ye dinna recognize these wolves? What did they look like? Did ye hear them speak? Hear an accent o' any kind?"

"There were three o' them. All big males, though no' as big as ye." He grinned as Cedric waved away his comment. But the truth was, his alpha was one the most respected pack leaders on three continents. Maybe more. And his size was only one part of it.

He continued his description. "Short locks on all three, dark as mine but a wee bit lighter than yers. Two were clean shaven and the other had fluff on his jaw, though nothin' tae write home aboot." Duncan gestured toward the fridge. Cedric nodded his permission and he walked over to grab something to drink. He opted for one of the waters. Though his alpha was known for drinking his Guinness, and alcohol burned off quickly in a shifter's system, Duncan preferred to keep a straight head this early in the day.

"Ye didn't hear them speak? Hear them say anything that would give us a clue as tae who they were?"

"Och. No. I dinna. They said no' a word. Just came in and started working th' place, splittin' up and searchin' th' crowd."

"But they dinna find who they were lookin' for?"

"No, they dinna." Because he may have rushed her out of there and barely escaped with their lives.

But, again, he didn't know this for sure. So, there was no point in bringing it up. Besides, once those wolves realized their prey—whoever that had been—had escaped, there'd be no need for them to stick around.

Cedric turned his head and gazed out the window. His expression was serene, but Duncan wasn't fooled. He could practically hear the sharp mind of his alpha whirring like a blender inside his skull. Wandering over to the couch, he made himself comfortable, and waited.

It wasn't long before Cedric turned around. "We need tae discover who these wolves are, and why they're here in my territory. With all we have goin' on with th' Fae, and with everything ye just told me, I dinna trust tha' they're just passin' through. I dinna ken who they are without more information, but they can no' just come here without permission and they

69

ken that. Which means they're up tae no good. Or they're tryin' tae cause trouble with this pack, and I dinna ken any wolf who is that *gallus* tae think they can just waltz on in here without me knowin'." He paused. "Ye said they saw ye, is tha' right?"

"Aye, they saw me." *Saw me hauling my arse down the highway.*

In spite of his promise to Ryanne, he was beginning to re-examine his reasons for not telling Cedric the whole story. What if they'd followed him back here? And something happened and the pack wasn't prepared because he'd neglected to mention the bonnie lass he'd rescued?

He sat forward, gripping his water in both hands, one knee bouncing up and down. "Cedric…"

A knock at the door interrupted his confession.

Cedric held up his finger for him to hold that thought and went to answer the door.

Duncan waited where he was, grateful for the interruption. It would give him time to think of a way to bring Ryanne into the picture without it sounding like he'd been purposely omitting her being there. Och. Maybe he should just admit to it. There was no harm done since he was telling him now.

"Prince Nada," Cedric said from the doorway. "What can I do fer ye?" The forced patience in his voice was almost comical.

"May I come in?"

Duncan smiled at his alpha's heavy sigh.

"Aye." He sounded less than thrilled.

The Fae prince strolled in, looking like he belonged in one of those fancy magazines. Impeccably groomed. Long, white hair. Black suit, silver cane, silver-toed boots.

Duncan vaguely wondered if he had an entire closetful of those suits, or just kept this one looking so clean and pressed with his Faerie woo-woo magic.

"Ah, Duncan. Good. Just the wolf I wanted to see."

A shiver of unease tingled down his spine. "Me?"

The prince smiled. "Yes. You. I heard you had a little excitement last night."

Cedric, having shut the door and now standing beside him, frowned. "How in th' hell would ye ken such a thing? Duncan was only just telling me."

The prince gave him an innocent look. "How is this my fault?"

"I dinna say it was yer fault. I said...Och. Never mind." Cedric huffed out a frustrated breath and took a seat in his new chair, nearly identical to the last one only it was tan, not blue. With a wave of his hand, he indicated the prince should carry on with what he was saying.

"As I was saying," Prince Nada continued. "I believe I know who these strange wolves were."

Duncan sat up, as did Cedric. "Ye do?"

"Yes." The prince looked around, eyeing the furniture before choosing to take a seat on the other end of the couch from Duncan. Laying his cane aside, he took a deep breath, settling back into the soft cushions.

Duncan focused on his breathing, keeping his heart

beating at a normal rhythm so Cedric wouldn't notice anything amiss.

The prince glanced over to the fireplace, cold and barren of wood, and gave a wistful sigh. "A fire would be very nice on a day like today. It's going to rain."

"It always rains here," Cedric told him.

Duncan watched as the prince stared at him for such a long time his fearless alpha began to squirm.

"Och, fine," he finally said, getting out of his chair. "I'll start a fire."

"No need to go through any trouble on my account," Prince Nada told him pleasantly. "It's really not that cold. But, thank you."

"Are ye going tae tell us?" Duncan asked to spare his alpha, who looked to be on the verge of having an apoplexy.

"Tell you what?" Prince Nada replied.

"Who th' wolves were I saw last night," he said.

"What wolves?"

"Och! The gods take me now!" Cedric exploded at the ceiling.

"Th' wolves," Duncan said at the same time. "Ye said ye ken who th' wolves are I saw last night at the club."

Prince Nada studied him closely. "I didn't know you were one to frequent those types of places."

"Aye. I like tae dance. Two Steppin' is my favorite."

"That's where ye go on yer nights off? Dancin'?" Cedric's mouth hung open.

But Duncan refused to feel any shame for something he enjoyed very much. Pushing his shoulders back, he gave them both a nod. "Aye. I go tae a place in Seattle and I like tae dance. It's a wonderful way tae meet th' ladies," he said with a wink.

"Tis like I dinna even know ye," Cedric muttered, still staring at Duncan as though he were seeing a ghost.

"Och, Cedric. I dinna ken why yer so surprised. I'm a good dancer!"

"Aye, I'm sure ye are. I just dinna ken ye ever took it up." He settled back into his chair again, sprawling out comfortably. "Ye usually tell me things such as this."

"I dinna tell ye—or anyone—because I was expecting just this type o' reaction."

"Wha'?" Cedric told him. "I told ye, I'm just surprised."

The prince, who'd been watching this interaction with interest, held his hand up to halt what Duncan had been about to say. "I'm sorry to interrupt, but can we get back to the matter at hand? Namely, the rogue wolves running around your territory. I know who they are, if either of you are interested in hearing."

Duncan exchanged a look with his alpha, beginning to feel his alpha's frustration with this royal pain in the ass. The male was right daft. A screwball. Off his head. And for sure should not be in charge of an entire tribe of Faeries. He would get them all killed when the portal holding the soul suckers broke free and another war broke out.

Sobered by the thought, he remembered that was exactly why they put up with the daft prince. They would need to work together to send the soul suckers back to the dimension they belonged in. And, hopefully, figure out how to keep them there this time.

"Aye, I would like tae ken who these wolves are. If ye feel so inclined tae tell us," Cedric told him.

How he kept such a level tone, Duncan didn't know.

The prince leaned forward, looking at each of them in turn like he was about to impart the secrets of life and death. "The wolves who followed you last night, Duncan, were from Thomas's pack back in the 'old country'. The same pack Lucian and Brock used to belong to."

Duncan felt his skin shift with unease on the back of his neck as Cedric speared him with those laser-sharp eyes of his. "They followed ye? Ye told me had no interest in ye."

"I was aboot tae tell ye when th' prince arrived," he tried to explain.

"Tell me what?"

"Don't you want to know *why* Thomas's wolves are here?" the prince asked.

But Cedric held up his hand. "Aye. But first I need tae ken why one o' my best wolves is tellin' me lies."

The weight of his disapproval descended on Duncan like one of those new weighted blankets times one hundred, and he found himself hunching over beneath his alpha's will. "Ye dinna need tae put th' pressure on, Cedric. I was aboot tae tell ye."

"Aye, ye are. And yer gonna do it right now. How far did they follow ye?"

"Dinna worry. I led them away from our home, into the

mountains, then doubled back when I was sure they would no' follow."

"Ye said they ignored ye at th' club," he repeated.

"They did."

"So, wha'? They did no' ken who ye were until ye left? That does no' make sense. If ye scented them right off, they would've done th' same with ye."

"They saw me. One o' them looked right at me."

"Then why did they feel th' need tae follow ye when ye left? And did no' say anything tae ye when they had th' safety o' a crowd o' humans around them?"

"It wasn't me they were following. It was th' lass I helped escape."

Cedric stilled. "Wha' lass?"

"I told ye on the phone I helped someone get out. What I did no' tell ye was that she was a Fae lass."

The prince leaned back against the couch cushions, raising one hand to his chest as though offended. "Faeries do not dance to country music."

"Aye, they do no'. And neither did this one," Duncan told him.

"Then what was she doing there?"

He tried to lie. He really did. She had asked him not to tell anyone about her, and when Duncan had sworn with everything in him that he would not say a word, he'd intended to keep that promise. But though he could've lied to the prince, it was impossible to do so against the will of his alpha. Duncan was a dominant wolf, but even he was no match for Cedric. "Watching me," he admitted. "She's been doin' it for some time now."

"What does this lass want with ye?" Cedric asked.

"I dinna ken. I think maybe she finds me…interesting?" He tried a smile. It didn't go over very well.

Cedric studied him carefully. "Ye dare tae criticize me, when ye yerself are off seducing a Faerie lass?"

He hurried to correct him. "Och, no, Cedric. Ye have it all wrong."

Cedric raised an eyebrow. "Yer tryin' tae tell me ye weren't flirtin' with this lass?"

"No. I was no'." For the gods sakes, he could barely form a coherent sentence when Ryanne was around. He couldn't flirt with her if he tried.

The thought gave him pause. What if something was wrong with him? The females always found him charming, and made it easy for him to be so. Why didn't this one?

"Then what exactly were you doing with her?" the prince asked. And though his expression gave nothing away, Duncan sensed more than the usual curiosity behind that question.

The pressure of both of their stares was heavy indeed, yet Duncan fought it as hard as he could. He'd already told them too much by admitting she was there at all.

"Duncan?"

Och. Cedric's will pressed upon him, threatening to crush his very bones if he didn't answer the question to his alpha's satisfaction.

And nothing but the truth would satisfy Cedric.

"I first saw her months ago, when Lucian and I were watching Keelin's house."

"Th' day ye saw Duana there?"

"Aye." He flicked a glance at the prince, but his highness was oddly quiet.

"Wha' was she doing there?"

"I dinna ken. When she saw I had spotted her, she ran off through th' forest."

"Ye did no' follow her?"

"No, I did no'."

"Why no'?"

He took a deep breath. He honestly didn't know why he hadn't tried to follow her. "I dinna ken."

Cedric sat back, and Duncan felt a little of the weight lift from his back. Not all of it, but enough that he could breathe deep again. Those white-blue eyes caught his. "And ye saw her again last night at th' club."

"Aye," he told him, hoping against hope he wouldn't pry any further.

But it was not to be. Cedric's gaze narrowed in on him, the oppression returning even heavier than before. "Tha' is no' th' only other time, is it?"

Duncan ground his teeth together so hard they began to ache. "No, Cedric."

"Dammit, Duncan!" Cedric exploded off the chair. "Do I have tae beat it out o' ye?"

Duncan jumped up also, and a low growl reverberated through the room. The response was automatic, and not one he'd ever had before toward his alpha.

Cedric stepped toward him, flashing his canines as his own growl rumbled from his chest. "Are ye challenging me, Duncan?"

He stared at his alpha. They were near the same size. Perhaps he could take him…

Duncan gave himself an internal shake. What in the holy hell was he doing? Over a lass he barely knew? He lowered his gaze and assumed a submissive stance. "No, Cedric. I apologize. I dinna ken what came over me."

As wolves ran hot, and so did their tempers, Cedric was quick to forgive him. However, Duncan knew he would not forget this. He had never come this close to challenging his alpha before. Not in all their years together.

Hands on his hips, Cedric sighed deep and long. "Duncan, ye need tae tell me what's going on. If Thomas's wolves are here and they're after that lass, and she has some need tae be near ye, she could verra well be endangering our pack. As could ye, by no' telling me th' truth."

Running a hand through his hair, Duncan nodded. Then he told him of the other times he'd seen her. Always miles from here or when he went into the city. No, he'd never seen her near their home. But that's not to say she didn't know where they lived.

"What did this 'lass' look like?" the prince asked, having finally decided to join the conversation.

"She has dark hair and eyes. Fair skin. Aboot this tall. Maybe a wee bit taller." He held his hand level just below his own shoulder.

"Did she tell you her name?"

Duncan glanced at Cedric. Something was telling him this was one thing he needed to hold firm about. Not to Cedric, but he did not want the prince to know any more than he already did.

He could not even tell himself the why of it.

With a look at his alpha he hoped he would understand, he answered the prince. "No. She did no'."

Ryanne. Her name came to him anyway. Sweet as the flowers she smelled like. At the thought of her, his entire body came to life, muscles hardening and his skin so sensitive he could feel the slightest change in the air around him. Emotions rolled through him as he repeated her name...

Ryanne.

But he was right not to tell the prince. It was nothing he could put his finger on, just a sense of truth that flowed through him sure as a river. Aye. Her name was one thing they would keep to themselves until they knew more about who she was and why she was there, and why Thomas's wolves had traveled so far to hunt her.

The prince tilted his head, eyes boring through Duncan's skull as though he could glean the truth from his brain that way. But everyone knew the Fae couldn't read minds.

Prince Nada's face suddenly went ashen. "Ryanne is ALIVE?"

Duncan had never seen the prince truly surprised about anything, until this very moment.

As a matter of fact, he looked nearly as surprised as Duncan himself was.

CHAPTER 7

"I did no' say her name," Duncan told him. Or had he? He glanced a Cedric in question.

Cedric gave a small shake of his head, confirming what Duncan already knew. The little hairs rose all over his body. A growl rose up in his chest, right behind Cedric's.

Fookin' Faeries and their fookin' magic. He could feel it permeating the room, thickening the air, and he stepped back, crossing himself and asking protection from the old gods. Or any god who was listening, really.

"I did no' say a name," he repeated to the prince. His blood burned hot, heating the back of his neck. He did *not* just break his promise to her.

Prince Nada stared at him hard.

Duncan felt worms crawling inside his brain, and he slammed his hands to either side of his head, trying to make it stop. The shift rolled beneath his skin. His wolf was angry. With a flash of his canines, he returned the prince's stare, daring him to dig out his thoughts if he could.

A flash of color lit the prince's eyes.

Wha' the fook was that?

"What are ye doin'?" Cedric stepped toward them. "I order ye tae stop it. Now! Do ye hear me?" His voice was little more than a growl, and Duncan knew his own wolf was fighting to break free.

With a loud snarl, Cedric stepped between the two males, breaking the connection.

Duncan released a harsh breath, bending at the waist, his head swimming as he tried to catch his breath. "I thought th' Fae were no' able tae read minds," he gritted out.

"They can't. Not normally," the prince said. His voice was almost robotic, like he was speaking on auto-pilot, not really realizing what he was saying. "Only ones who are very, very old can catch things sometimes, and only if there is a lot of emotion beneath the thought."

Cedric grabbed Duncan by the shoulders and pulled him upright. "What th' fook is going on, Duncan?"

"I was tryin' tae tell ye…"

"Tell me more about my daughter." The prince sank onto the closest couch cushion.

A shock of surprise knocked the air right back out of Duncan as Cedric stilled beside him. "Yer what?"

Still looking shell-shocked, the prince's eyes gradually wandered over to him. "My daughter. Ryanne. That is who saw last night, yes? That's who has been following you? She has dark, curly hair, dark eyes, and the refined features of a

Faerie princess." A wistful smile teased the corners of his mouth. "Because that's exactly what she is. Next in line to take the throne."

"Ye actually have a throne?" Duncan asked.

"Aye," Cedric told him. He crossed his arms over his wide chest. "I saw it once when I was summoned tae his house. He and Duana. Though hers was much smaller."

In that same strange voice, the prince said, "She's not going to give it up easily." He looked at Cedric. "Her throne." Then he stood up, clasped his hands behind his back, and began to pace back and forth, staring at the floor beneath his fancy boots. "This changes everything. And yet, it needs to change nothing."

Duncan watched him walk back and forth in front of the fireplace, and the more time that passed, the more uneasy he felt.

Prince Nada suddenly stopped, turned, and marched up to Duncan. Cedric growled low in his throat, stepping up to intercept, but Duncan held out his arm, stopping him. He wanted to hear what the prince had to say.

"You're sure it was my daughter? It was Ryanne? And don't bother trying to lie, wolf. I've been inside your mind."

"Then why are ye askin'? If ye already ken th' truth."

Tilting his head to the side, the prince studied him. "I don't really know. I guess I'm just finding it hard to believe. My daughter, you see, is dead. She died during the first war. Taken out by one of your kind."

For a moment, he couldn't speak. If Ryanne was dead, who the fook had he gotten out of the club last night? For the female he'd held in his arms was no ghost, but warm flesh and strong bone and soft, pretty things. And bodies that were decaying did not smell like primrose. "Tha' would no' have happened," Duncan told him. "The wolves were on yer side. Why would anyone have harmed your wee daughter?"

In answer, the prince smiled. It was a creepy smile. And Duncan barely resisted the urge to cross himself again, though he couldn't repress the slight shiver that shook him from the top of his head down to the soles of his feet, despite the warm cotton shirt he was wearing.

"Why, indeed?" Prince Nada asked. He turned and paced away, and Duncan exchanged another look with Cedric.

"Is this who you've been messing around with? Th' fookin' prince's daughter?"

Though Cedric spoke in no more than a whisper, Duncan had no problem hearing the censure in his tone. "I dinna 'mess around' with th' lass. I just got her out o' th' club and took her somewhere safe."

"You're no' going tae tell me where tha' is, are ye?"

"No' right now, no." He kept one eye on the prince, who was now having a full-blown conversation in the corner of the room with no one Duncan could see. "I will. As soon as this one is on his way."

"Aye. Yer damned right ye will," Cedric confirmed.

Duncan kept his eyes downcast, but he refused to accept he'd done anything wrong. He'd for sure been about to tell him about the lass, and he wouldn't be shamed into thinking he'd done wrong by his alpha because this one—he shot a glare at the prince—showed up blathering about things that no one was ready to tell him and stealing thoughts right from his head that he had no business to take.

Prince Nada suddenly stilled and turned to them. "This will not do. This will not do at all. Ryanne is supposed to be dead. And I can't have her rising from the grave like this to upset all of my plans."

Duncan's heart jumped to his throat. "What is tha' supposed tae mean?" he asked him.

"Hmm?" The prince looked up, frowning at him and Cedric as though he'd forgotten they were there, despite the fact he was looking right at them both. "Oh…nothing."

Duncan turned to his alpha. "Cedric…"

"Wait a minute." Cedric stepped in front of the prince as he made to leave. "Ye are no' planning on bringing harm tae th' lass, are ye? Yer own flesh and blood daughter? Have ye no heart?"

"Not all species of the supernatural are as sensitive to our emotions as yours, wolf."

"Dinna give me tha'. It's rubbish, and ye ken it. She is yer daughter. Yer own flesh and blood."

"You're right, Cedric. I care deeply about my daughter, but I care about the survival of my people more." He looked back over his shoulder at Duncan. "I will find her, and she will trouble you no longer." He started to walk around Cedric, stopped, snapped his fingers, and returned to the couch to retrieve his cane.

Duncan was having a hard time processing what he had just heard.

As he passed, the prince paused just long enough to tell him, "It was good of you to keep her safe. If Thomas's wolves had gotten a hold of her, she would've suffered a horrendous death. At least this way, when I send her back where she belongs, it will be quick…and relatively painless. So, thank you for sparing my daughter that." With a nod at Cedric, he walked away, disappearing before he even reached the door.

A storm of emotions rolled over Duncan, crashing through the shock and spurring him into action. He pointed at the space the prince had just stood. "He's going tae kill her, Cedric! His own fookin' daughter!" Stalking to the door, he stopped, spun back. "I can no' let him do this." He ripped at his hair. "Fook me! I dinna ken where she is, or how tae warn her." Rage and fear tangled in his gut, intertwining like two mating snakes until he shook with the force of it.

"He's no' going tae hurt th' lass, Duncan."

"Aye, he is!"

"No, he is no'. Because we will find her first and we will warn her. Now, fill me in again on everything tha' happened last night, and dinna leave anything out this time."

Some of Cedric's calm, focused disposition finally managed to spill over into Duncan and he forced himself to think. With measured words, he told Cedric everything. From the moment he first saw her until she hopped out of his Jeep last night. When he was finished, he looked to his alpha, at a loss. "I dinna ken where she went. and I should no' even be telling ye this. I swore it tae her. Now she's in danger, because o' me!"

"No' because o' ye, because tha' galoot can no' stay out o' our business. It's like he has cameras watching us all th' time, so he kens when we're speaking o' anything important tae him." He shook his head. "No. He is no' going tae hurt this lass just because he had plans tha' did no' include her."

It hit Duncan like a truck. "Like him marrying Duana off tae ye."

"Aye," Cedric agreed. "Like tha'." He took a deep breath. "Though I can no', for the life o' me, figure out why the daft prince wants such a mating."

Duncan felt torn in every direction, not knowing what to do or where to go. "What should I do, Cedric?"

His alpha studied him long and hard. "Why am I gettin' th' feeling this lass means a lot more tae ye than yer telling me." It wasn't really a question.

"I barely know th' lass, Cedric," Duncan told him honestly. "I dinna ken wha' I'm feeling."

"But it is something."

Words and thoughts and things he had no name for churned through his mind, none of it making any sense. Except one thing: "It does no' matter, Cedric. I would no' be any kind o' mate for th' lass." He held his head high as he said it.

"Duncan, ye dinna ken tha'."

"Except I do. And I'm no' ashamed o' it, Cedric. Wha' happened tae me was no' something any male should ever tae withstand. And ye ken I dinna blame any but th' ones who did it tae me."

"It was war. We all went through things. It does no' mean yer no' a male anymore."

"Aye, yer right. But it does mean I would no' make a decent mate for any lass. And especially no' this lass in particular. I do no' blame her. She was no' there. But I dinna ken if I could ever be tha' vulnerable around one of the Fae." There was no shame in his words. Cedric knew everything there was to know about him. And he'd spoken the truth when he said he didn't blame all of the Fae for what happened to him so many years ago.

"She's no' one o' them, Duncan. She's no' *an olc.*"

He scrubbed his face with his hands, then dropped them to his hips as he thought about what Cedric was saying. "I dinna think it matters. My head does no' differentiate between th' tribes. No' when it comes tae something so personal as trusting her with my heart and soul."

Cedric laid a heavy hand on his shoulder. "Ye may no' have th' choice, my friend. Th' heart wants who th' heart wants, and I feart yers has already made up its mind."

"Och, Cedric." He tried to lighten the mood. "My heart kens nothing o' th' sort. Ye ken it's a fickle beast."

But his alpha knew him best of anyone and wasn't taking the bait. "I dinna want tae see ye alone th' rest o' yer days. If ye feel pulled tae this lass, ye should at least give her a chance."

Duncan placed his hand on Cedric's shoulder, mimicking his alpha's pose. "I will no' be alone. I have ye." Giving him a wink, he grinned.

"Hmph," Cedric chuckled. Then he grabbed Duncan by the back of the head and touched their foreheads together briefly before releasing him. "In any case, we can no' let th' prince find th' lass before we do. Let's call th' rest o' th' pack in. We will only tell them aboot last night, no' th' rest o' it. We will take shifts searching th' forest, and ye can keep an eye around th' club."

"Even ye, Cedric?"

"Aye. Even me. After all, I can no' let anything happen tae my best *mukker's* mate."

"Och. She's no' my mate."

Cedric smiled, but only briefly. "Just…think aboot what I said Duncan."

Another joke hovered on the edge of his tongue, but catching Cedric's steady stare, Duncan let it die. "Aye. I'll think on it."

"Good." Cedric smacked him on the ass. "Now, get out yer cell and round up th' others. I want everyone here in ten minutes."

Duncan pulled out his phone, but paused with his thumbs above the keyboard. If they pulled everyone in on the search, it would alert the lass for sure. She might even run before he could warn her. "Cedric, I'd like tae have the chance tae try finding her on my own first. I dinna want her tae get spooked."

Cedric gave him a thoughtful look. "Aye, ye might be right there." He gave Duncan a nod. "Ye have four days. If ye can no' find the lass by then, I'm calling in the others tae help ye. In the meantime, I'll double up the patrols around the area and be sure tae tell everyone tae keep an eye out for any strange wolves."

"Thank ye, Cedric. I'll find her."

"Ye better," his alpha told him.

Aye, Duncan thought. He didn't know how, but he would find the lass before the daft prince.

He had to.

CHAPTER 8

R yanne swore to herself she would leave the wolf alone. And she never broke her promises to herself. Not ever.

Except, apparently, just this once.

From the cover of the trees, she watched him climb up into his vehicle and drive away. And by the way he was dressed, she could guess exactly where he was going.

But why would he be going there? It was only a week ago they'd made their great escape from those non-resident wolves. Surely, they were still lurking around.

However, she was not a female who cowered from danger—or who liked to miss out on the fun. Especially when it could help her find out why her father was hanging around with werewolves when the war had been over for years.

Lucky for her, she'd left her cozy, little cabin and had

gone shopping in the city the day before, so she had just the thing to wear.

Ryanne backed away from the tree line carefully, eyes and ears alert to any unexpected company. Duncan's pack had been more active than normal, roaming the forest every hour of the day and night until a Faerie could barely move without tripping over one of them.

Once or twice she thought maybe she'd been scented, but she didn't worry overmuch about it. They would never see her unless she wanted to be seen.

The three they'd seen last week, however, had been conspicuously absent from the area. She wondered if this was why Duncan was heading back there. Did he think it was safe? Or was he hoping to find them?

If it was the second option, Ryanne was definitely joining him. And this time, if the humans would behave, perhaps she could find out what it was they wanted from her. Although it was possible they were just extremely anti-Faerie, and she'd just been in the wrong place at the wrong time, somehow she seriously doubted that was the case, and this was what she needed to find out.

Besides, they couldn't very well hurt her or drag her forcibly out of the club without attracting undo notice from the humans. And since they greatly outnumbered both of their own kind, that was something best avoided for the good of all. So, if she could keep them in the club, it was completely possible she could engage them in conversation and find out what was what. Especially if Duncan was there to back her up.

Making her way back to her borrowed cabin, she changed into the clothes she'd lifted from a retail shop yesterday. Ryanne had the money to pay for it, but it was always good to keep her foraging skills sharp. Just in case.

The dress was a soft, creamy white with little blue flowers all over it. Loose and flowing, it moved when she did and was much more comfortable than the denim she normally wore, if less sparkly. It even had pockets she could fit her whole hand in.

Her new boots were in the cowboy style, calf high, dark brown, with bling around the top and throughout the threaded design to make up for the lack of embellishments on her dress. Sparkly things made her happy, and she rarely went a day without wearing something that shined. Pulling her hair into a high ponytail, she twisted a few shorter curls around her finger and left them hanging around her face. She was tempted to try the face paint human women were so fond of, but in the end, she only applied a shiny pink gloss to her lips.

It tasted like coconuts.

Outside, she left a pile of peanuts for her friend in case she didn't make it back in a timely manner, and then, with a glance at the sky, she decided to walk.

Or rather, run.

A bubble of laughter escaped as she dodged thick tree trunks and the wet leaves of ferns. She ran so fast no eye would be able to track her, not even a shifter's. To anyone else, she was something they thought they saw out of the corner of their eye. There and gone again. Leaving them unsure they'd seen anything at all.

Ryanne threw her arms out to the side, feeling the wind rush by her, flushing her cheeks and tangling in her hair. Her breath was even in her lungs, her skin damp only from the moist air. The spice of pine trees and the musk of furry animals and damp earth filled her nose.

Freedom, she thought to herself, was one of the most wonderful things. And on this night, she felt truly free for the first time in a long time.

She took her time getting to the city, arriving on foot about forty minutes after Duncan. Smiling at the bouncer, he gestured for her to go in without paying the cover. He was horribly biased toward pretty females, but it worked in her favor, so she didn't bother telling him that kind of behavior wasn't acceptable in this day and age. The human women didn't appear to mind, so why should she?

The shifter found her the moment she walked in. He was sitting at the end of the bar closest to the door, and so she saw the moment he scented her, his head whipping around, green eyes so intense it made her catch her breath when they zeroed in on her like a magical arrow finding its target.

Without further ado, he slammed his beer down onto the bar and marched up to her.

"Ye did no' tell me yer th' daughter o' Prince Nada."

Ryanne took a moment to breathe in his earthy masculine scent, tinged only slightly with the beer he'd been drinking. It was altogether quite a pleasant smell to her. Almost as good as the forest. "Does it matter?"

"Aye. Aye, it does matter."

"Why?"

That threw him off. He took a step back. "Because ye dinna tell me."

"So, I'm supposed to tell you everything?"

"Aye."

She cocked her head, studying this shifter who felt so entitled to her thoughts and her person. Although, if she were to be honest with herself, she was just as interested in his...person. "How did you find out who I am?"

A new song came through the speakers overhead, and a female with a pleasant voice starting singing, asking the crowd how she could live without her love. The lyrics brought a surge of emotion to the surface, catching Ryanne off guard, although she couldn't have said why.

"Music has a way o' touching yer soul," Duncan murmured so low no one else would be able to hear.

Her eyes flew to his. How did he know what was happening inside of her? Almost better than she did, it seemed. It's not like she hadn't heard sad songs before. Ryanne had been alive and living in this world for a long, long time. Of course, she had. She'd heard them in this club. But honestly, she'd never really paid much attention to them, preferring to listen to the songs of nature. The wind through the trees. A bird's morning song. Frogs serenading her to sleep with their deep, throaty voices.

Even the howl of the wolves.

"Dance with me."

Pulled from her musings, Ryanne frowned. The thought

of being held so close to him disturbed her. The last time it happened, when he'd taken her from the club during the fight, it had made her feel...not like herself. "Oh, I don't know how to do that."

"But I do. Ye have nothing tae worry aboot. I'll show ye." Taking her hand, he tugged her toward the crowded dance floor where couples shuffled around in a circle, some of them already quite noticeably drunk and using their partner to prop them up.

Or, perhaps they just liked being wrapped around each other like that.

Ryanne let him lead her out to the floor. She'd never danced with a male like this, so up close and personal. And certainly not with a shifter. She'd never understood the need to cuddle. Unless she was in the act of having sex, she preferred no one in her personal space.

When he reached the edge of the circle, he lifted the hand he was holding to his shoulder and placed his on her waist. Catching her other hand, he laced his fingers through hers and brought their combined hands in close to his chest. "Just do wha' I do, only with th' opposite foot."

Duncan then started shuffling backward. Two steps with one foot, one with the other. Repeat.

Ryanne kept her eyes on his boots for a single turn around the floor, picking up the rhythm easily as he maneuvered them through the crowd of other couples.

"Och. Yer a natural."

She looked up to see him grinning down at her. It was

the first true smile she'd seen from him. At least one that was aimed at her. One untainted by stress or distractions.

And now, to be the receiver of that smile...gods, she was not prepared. The breath whooshed from her lungs, and she felt a moment of lightheadedness. Caught up in that smile, Ryanne's steps faltered, but she caught herself with a little direction from his hand on her back.

Ryanne had never met a male she considered irresistible, although she would readily admit some were more appealing than others. Some had a pleasant face. Some had a goodness within them that made them more attractive despite the features mother nature gave them. And some had just the opposite—a face and body that caught a woman's eye right away, but who spewed hateful or chauvinist words that made her roll them away again just as quickly.

She had yet to meet a male who caused her to lose her breath with nothing but a smile. A smile that transformed his handsome face into something...more.

Until this very moment.

As she stared up at him, the grin slowly melted away. The teasing twinkle in his green eyes fading, to be replaced by an inner luminance that burned with a heat so hot she could feel it burn her all the way to her soul.

He pulled her in closer, molding her curves to his hardness until she was barely conscious of dancing. With every step, her breasts pressed against his chest, and his hand moved down her back to hold her hips tight to his. Only their legs brushed as they stepped around the dance floor

In that moment, they could've been the only ones on the floor.

As she looked up at him, Ryanne's mouth was only inches from his, and she couldn't help but wonder what would it feel like to kiss him?

"Ye look…in that dress, ye look…" He shook his head. "I was going tae say 'bonnie', but that's no' th' word." His eyes released hers, dipping to her nose, her cheek, her jaw… leaving the scorch of his burning stare everywhere they touched. "Dazzling," he finally said in a faraway voice. "Aye." He nodded slightly, sounding more certain now. "Ye look dazzling tonight, Ryanne."

Ryanne had received praise on her appearance before from the cowboys in this place, but never had anyone called her "dazzling". "Thank you," she murmured, truly touched. Because it wasn't a practiced compliment. It wasn't a line from a human so he could dip his dick. It was something honest coming from a pure place inside of him. But he looked so rapt as he stared down at her, she couldn't resist teasing him. "Do you even remember what I'm wearing?"

"Aye. A dress with wee blue flowers that hugs yer curves when ye move. But it does no' matter what ye wear," he told her. "Ye shine from within, lass. Ye could be covered in nothing but the mud of the earth and ye would still shine like an angel." With noticeable effort, he pulled his eyes from her face and glanced back over his shoulder to direct them around an older, slower couple as a blush crept up his neck. "Maybe it's th' Faerie magic inside o' ye," he murmured low.

She immediately missed the heat of his eyes on her face, but she was also grateful to be out from underneath the intensity of his stare so she could breathe again. It took her a few steps before she could speak again. "Do you know many Faeries?"

He glanced back at her. "Aye. A few."

"And they all have this inner glow, then?" She smiled at him.

His steps slowed as he contemplated her question while those bright eyes again roamed over her face and hair. "No," he said. He sounded surprised by his own answer. "No, they dinna."

She didn't know what to say to that.

They took another turn around the floor in silence, and Ryanne found herself as enraptured by him as he seemed to be with her. Up close like this, she could see the laugh lines around his eyes, a little lighter than his olive-toned skin. Shallow creases from his smile carved his face on either side of his mouth. His lips were not too thin, not too full, and had just enough color to them. His dark hair was cut short and fell naturally around his head, a few pieces covering the upper part of his forehead. His skin was a bit weathered. His jawline strong. A manly face. An attractive face.

"Ye should no' have come here, Ryanne."

The "R" of her name rolled off his tongue in his Scottish brogue. She'd never been overly fond of the name, but it sounded beautiful when he said it. "Why not?"

The music changed to something faster, and with obvious reluctance he released her. Taking her hand, he led her from the dance floor and over to the bar where he tucked her into a corner stool and stood beside her, his back to the door so no one coming in would see her.

She smiled to herself at his protective gesture. Wolves, by nature, did not like their backs turned to possible threats.

"Because I came here lookin' for ye," he told her. "And because it's verra likely those wolves who chased us will come back here looking for ye, tae. And ye shouldn't be here when they do."

"But that's what I'm hoping for," she told him. "I have questions."

"Aye, so do I." He waved down the bartender, an attractive brunette he barely glanced at. "Would ye like a drink?"

"A gin and tonic, please," she told the bartender, then turned back to Duncan.

He frowned. "So, ye came here tae risk yer life again?"

The bartender set her drink and his beer on the counter. Ryanne picked it up and took a sip. "I came here to find a wolf," she told him honestly.

And it suddenly struck her that she'd found who it was she was looking for.

CHAPTER 9

Duncan searched her wee face, as he had the feeling she wasn't taking this as seriously as she should be, and found her brown eyes dancing with humor. Or was it something else?

Och, it didn't matter. Did the lass not realize the danger she was in?

"Ye should no' have come," he told her again. "They could come back here searching for ye."

She arched one brow. "So, I should leave?"

"Och, no," he said in a rush. Snapping his jaws shut, he tried his best to recover. "Yer here now. Ye may as well stay for a bit."

"So glad I have your approval," she told him.

He glanced at her to see if she was teasing again. She was not. Why the fook couldn't he say anything right around her? He spoke with females on a daily basis. As a matter of fact, they'd always given him the impression of being rather fond of conversing with him. He could even make them giggle, which he rather liked the sound of, and it sure didn't hurt anything to make a female feel good about herself. The world would go to shit without them. Every decent male knew and accepted that fact.

Duncan glanced around them, checking that none of Thomas's wolves had snuck in when he wasn't looking. He didn't trust himself to catch them by scent or instinct alone, not when he was so flustered by the creature perched on the stool in front of him. Not because she bedazzled him, although every word he'd told her earlier was true. But because he needed answers. And it was hard to concentrate on getting those answers when she was tripping him up every time he tried by looking at him with those bonnie eyes and smiling at him with those bonnie lips.

Not to mention how her sweet primrose scent filled his nose until all he could think about was having that smell all over him.

And because he needed to tell her that he had utterly failed at keeping her secret. That although he'd had every intention to, he'd had no choice in the matter. Och, he was not looking forward to that. No' at all. Ryanne had trusted him to keep her secret. And he'd broken that trust before twenty-four hours had gone by. What kind of a friend— what kind of a male—did that make him?

"So." She set her half-empty glass down on the bar. "How many people exactly did you tell? About my being here?" she clarified.

His eyes widened. "Wha' makes ye think I told anyone?"

"You're staring at me with such a guilty look on your face, I assume you either told someone or you just accidentally ran over my cat. And as far as I know, I don't have a cat. And if I did, I certainly wouldn't be letting it run around loose where it could get run over."

Duncan released a long breath and hung his head in shame. "I dinna mean tae do it. I swear tae ye, I didn't. It was torn from me against my will." He sighed, rubbing at a worn spot on the bar with his fingertips as he tried to think of how to explain it to her. "Ye have tae ken how it is with wolves. Within the pack, I mean." He gave her an imploring look and pressed on. "I'm no' th' alpha. and I did no' have a choice."

"You're dominant enough to be an alpha," she commented offhandedly.

Pride filled his chest and pushed his shoulders back. "Aye. I am." Then he shook his head. "But tha's no' th' point. I'm no' th' alpha, Cedric is. And when he wants tae ken something, there's no hiding it from him."

"And that's how you found out I'm the prince's daughter," she said.

"Aye." Sort of.

"But how does your alpha—Cedric, is it?—know who I am?"

She watched him carefully for his answer, and Duncan got the impression he'd better tread with the utmost caution if he wanted any chance at all of regaining her trust. And it was important for him to do so, though he wasn't quite sure of the why of it. He just knew it was.

"I did no' mention yer name to Cedric. I swear it tae ye. I never said it aloud."

"Then how did he hear it?"

"Someone else was there, and he…" What? Guessed? Read his mind? "He knew," he finished lamely. "He just knew. Because ye were in my head."

Instead of the angry sparks he'd expected, her eyes softened, turning from icy tundra to the color of warm autumn.

It made him nervous. And suspicious. "Wha'?" he asked. Smooth. Very smooth. At least he hadn't stuttered.

"So, you were thinking of me."

He frowned. "O' course I was thinking o' ye. I was in th' middle o' telling Cedric aboot th' wolves. Ye were there. And I was tryin' tae tell it like ye weren't. So, I had tae think o' ye so I wouldn't speak o' ye." Somehow, that made much more sense in his head.

"But someone read your mind." She smiled a secretive smile.

He released his breath. "Aye."

"Let me guess. Prince Nada, princely prince of the 'good' Faeries." She made air quotes, then rolled her eyes and took another long drink, set her empty glass on the bar, and flagged down the bartender for another.

Duncan watched all of this distractedly. "Why does yer da think yer dead?" he blurted.

"Because I was."

He suppressed the need to cross himself. Was this a ghost he was speaking to? But no, that couldn't be true. A ghost wouldn't have filled his arms the way she had when they'd danced just a few minutes ago. However, to be certain, he reached out and touch her arm where it lay on the bar, just to reassure himself she was still warm flesh and blood.

His fingers tingled as they connected with her bare skin, and reluctantly, he pulled them away. The same thing had happened when he'd taken her hand to dance. Like something inside of her was trying to connect with something inside of him. He didn't know what it was, or what to think about it. This had never happened to him before, not with any female he'd ever been around. And he was often around females.

She looked down at her drink as she stirred it. "So, what did my father say when he pulled me from your head?"

Duncan shook himself, refocusing on their conversation with effort. Her tone was deceptively casual, but he had a gut feeling she wasn't as unaffected as she was trying to let on. "He was surprised you're alive, and..." He drifted off, not knowing how to tell her that her own father wasn't happy to find out she was still breathing.

She cocked her head, studying him until his face burned with the lies he was tempted to utter. But then she said, "It's okay, wolf. You can tell me the truth. Actually, I prefer it. It's always good to know where one stands, and there's no love lost between the male who sired me and myself." She brought her drink up to her lips. "Trust me," she muttered right before she took a sip.

Duncan searched her face and saw nothing but honesty in her expression this time. "He said..." He stopped. He couldn't say it out loud. "Och. Dinna make me say it, lass." Grabbing the beer he'd just realized was by his elbow, he took a long swallow.

"He wasn't happy that I'd come back from the dead, was he?" She lifted her chin, her voice strong, as though she didn't care in the least what the prince thought.

But Duncan could see the sadness beneath the brave façade. He shook his head. "I'm sorry, lass." And then he forced himself to tell her. "He wants tae send ye back tae th' grave. So as no' tae mess up his plans."

There was no reaction to his words other than a brief pause when she lowered her eyes before she raised them back to his. "And what plans are those?"

"Tae have Duana mated tae my alpha, and for her tae be next in line tae take th' crown."

"Duana? The princess?"

"Aye."

She turned her head, watching the dancers in the mirror behind the bar. "Well, he won't be getting that wish, Duncan."

"I sincerely hope not, Ryanne."

They sat in silence for a few minutes as he let her stew on all he had just told her. And the longer he sat there, the angrier he became. How could anyone want to kill their own child? Their own flesh and blood?

He would have to be a psychotic bastard. Worse than any of them had presumed. If Duncan were ever so lucky to have such a miracle bestowed upon him, if he ever sired a bairn, nothing and no one would ever get close enough to that babe to cause them any harm. No matter how old they were.

"Did you find out who the wolves were that chased us?" she asked after a time.

"Aye. They belong to a pack from Scotland."

She turned to look at him, one side of her mouth quirked up with amusement. "Thomas's pack?"

"Aye, that would be th' one." He watched her go back to watching the dancers. "Ye dinna seem concerned."

"I'm not," she said.

"Ye ken this pack?"

"I do."

"Why are they after ye?"

"Because they also know who I am. And, they also want me dead."

"What for? What did ye do tae Thomas?"

"Not a thing, except be what I am. But he and my father have known each other a long, long time." She barked out a laugh. "It wouldn't surprise me if they're here because my father asked them to come here."

"I dinna believe that," he told her. "The prince was genuinely shocked tae find out."

"That makes no sense." She tapped her fingers on the bar. "The prince might be playing you, making you believe what he wants you to believe. What would Thomas's wolves be doing here otherwise?"

Duncan thought perhaps he knew. But it was not his business to tell. It would be Lucian's. "They might be here for a completely different reason altogether, and maybe running into ye here was as much a surprise tae them as it was tae yer da."

"Thomas thinks the only good Faerie is a dead Faerie," she said more to herself than to him. "Much like all of you wolves did. Before."

"Before the war."

Her eyes flew to his. "Yes."

But he only shook his head. "'Tis no' true now." She didn't seem to believe him, but it wasn't something he'd be able to convince her of with words. This he knew. It would have to be something she experienced for herself. "However, Thomas seems tae think he can do as he please, wherever he pleases."

"He's always been a bit full of himself."

"Aye," he agreed. Duncan had never met the Scottish alpha, but he'd heard stories from both Lucian and now Brock. "So, perhaps ye can tell me, is there anyone who does no' want tae kill ye?"

She gave him a brilliant smile. "There's you."

Aye. She was right, there. He did not want to harm a wee hair on her bonnie head. He felt it would break his heart to do so—as soon as it began beating again after she stopped it with that smile—which made not a lick of sense, as he barely knew the lass.

Yet…he felt like their souls had touched before. Like he did, in fact, know her. The sound of her laugh, the feel of her eyes on him, the dips and valleys of her curves. The slide of her skin on his…

The warm glow of her love.

But that was impossible. Because he'd never been that close to anyone before the war. And after…

Well, after the war, things are different. They would want a true mate. Something Duncan could never be now.

Ryanne slammed her glass down on the bar top, jarring him from his melancholy thoughts. "Come on, wolf."

Never one to dwell on things that couldn't be changed, he picked up his beer and chugged down the remainder in two swallows. Wiping his mouth on the napkin it was on, he then set both back on the bar. "Where are we goin'?"

"Somewhere else," was all she would tell him. "I'm getting tired of glaring at all the human females who keep walking by trying to catch your attention."

What? He looked to his left. Sure enough, Daisy, Elma and Jessica were giving him curious glances as they clustered around a tall table nearby. Daisy even gave him a little wave.

He grinned, winked, and waved back. He meant nothing by it. It was an automatic reaction.

The sound of Ryanne clearing her throat reminded him that his company was spoken for, at least for the moment. Tingles danced up his arm as Ryanne grabbed his hand and pulled him out of the bar, and the human females were forgotten.

When they got outside, he pulled her to a stop, making her wait while he smelled the night air for any scents that didn't belong. But there was no sign of the shifters. Only the normal scents of unwashed homeless bodies, greasy restaurants, car emissions, wet pavement, and the faint, salty taste of the nearby sea.

Ryanne stood patiently by his side and waited. "All safe?" she asked when he started walking again.

Duncan glanced down at her. One corner of her mouth was twitching, like she was fighting a smile. "Dinna laugh at me." He tapped the side of his nose. "Ye will be happy for this when it saves ye from being ambushed by three angry wolves determined tae get their paws on ye."

They got to the Vina, and as he fished around in his pocket for his keys, he was surprised to hear her say, "You're right. I shouldn't laugh at you. Especially after what you did for me the last time."

He found his keys and unlocked his door. "So, where are we goin', lass?" When she didn't respond, he turned to her, keys dangling from his fingers.

She was staring at him strangely.

"Wha'?" he asked.

Her eyes narrowed in on his mouth. "Duncan?"

"Aye?"

"Why have you never tried to kiss me?"

He looked at her perfect, bonnie lips and his breath caught in his lungs. Och. He wanted to. The lass had no idea how much he wanted to. But..."It's no' that I dinna want tae."

"Are you afraid of me?"

"No," he answered immediately. But the word tripped on his tongue. "No," he told her more forcefully. "I am no'."

She stepped closer, and Duncan forced himself to hold his ground. He wasn't afraid of a wee Faerie lass.

"I want to kiss you," she said.

Before he could think of an argument as to why they shouldn't do this, Duncan found himself with his back pressed against the side of his Jeep. Soft, womanly curves held him prisoner better than any steel bars ever could, and he knew, in that moment, how his mated brothers had never stood a chance against a Fae lass.

Staring down at her, he tried again to come up with a good reason as to why they shouldn't do this even though his heart was pounding near out of his chest and the air was having a hell of a time getting into his lungs. But all he could manage was, "I can no', Ryanne." The words were little more than a whisper.

"I think you can, wolf."

He gritted his teeth and shook his head back and forth.

She nodded hers. Then she put her hands behind his neck and pulled his head down until they were eye to eye. "I need to get you out of my system," she whispered, so close he felt her words against his mouth more than heard them. "You're distracting me from killing my father."

He had no time to absorb what she'd just said, for then her lips were pressed to his, moving against his mouth insistently. Duncan growled low in his throat as her tongue swept in to tangle with his, and his fingers dug into the hard sides of the vehicle.

He ached to hold her. Ached all the way down to his soul.

Ached to wrap his arms around her and pull her in so tight neither of them would know where one stopped and the other began. And by the way she was biting at his lips and digging her fingers into the back of his neck, she wanted the same. But he couldn't do it. It would be nothing but torture for him to hold her, knowing that's all he would ever be able to do.

Instead, he forced himself to turn his head, breaking the kiss, and then, unable to stand even that much distance between them, pressed his cheek against hers. He fought to get his breathing under control enough so he was able to speak. "I can no' do this, lass," he whispered. "Please do no' force me tae. Ye will break me like nothing else." And this was something he knew in his bones, though he could not have said how.

She pulled away, her wee hands letting up just enough that she could look into his face. But Duncan kept his eyes downcast. He couldn't look at her. Heat suffused his face as his muscles began to tremble with the urge to run. Run away from this female who made him wish so desperately for things he couldn't have.

"Duncan..."

"Please dinna make me confess things tae ye, Ryanne. I could no' stand it if ye looked upon me as any less o' a male." He clenched his jaw so hard his teeth ached and fought to swallow around the lump in his throat, fighting the surge of loneliness that assailed him as she pulled away. Loneliness he had no business feeling.

He stayed as he was for long seconds, muscles tense,

fighting his own cowardice. He wanted to jump into the Jeep and drive away. Run as far as he could.

But he would not, could not, leave her here like that.

Finally, she said, "I would appreciate a ride, if the offer is there."

He exhaled long and slow. "Aye," he said, sadly. "O' course it is."

"Okay. Thank you." But she stayed where she was. "Duncan…"

He squeezed his eyes shut, the pain like a clamp around his chest. "Please, Ryanne. Do no'. I beg o' ye."

A few seconds later, he heard her boots walking away from him as she went to the other side of the Jeep. He tried to inhale, to take a breath, but the loss of her was like ripping the skin from his body.

Twisting his head to either side until he felt the bones pop in his neck and his wolf settle down again, he shot a look around the lot, but thankfully it was empty.

One hand on the door handle, he took a shaky breath. Then he yanked open the door and climbed in.

CHAPTER 10

Ryanne watched the wolf from the corner of her eye as they cruised east down the highway away from Seattle. She expected to see more of a reaction from him, but although he was quiet, he otherwise appeared perfectly at ease. There was no indication he felt the least bit uncomfortable after the intimate moment they'd just shared together.

Or rather, his strange reaction to it.

His hands didn't grip the steering wheel too tightly. His jaw was no longer clenched. He didn't appear sad, or uneasy. And, although he still wouldn't look at her, he was humming under his breath. She recognized it as the song they had danced to.

She didn't understand. He was attracted to her, as much or more so than she was him. When she'd kissed him, his hunger for more had been a palpable thing, rolling off his body like a wave of flames to stoke her own desire. Yet, he'd refused to touch her. Refused to hold her. Only devoured her with his lips and tongue as she had him until he'd abruptly pulled away.

So, why had he stopped?

Her curiosity was peaked. Rejection was not something Ryanne was used to, and it was not something she was about to accept from a male who clearly wanted her. However, it was becoming clear he had more than a few demons inside of him. And, strangely enough, Ryanne was moved by his inner battle with them. Perhaps she could help this shifter who'd been nothing but kind to her.

But, for now, maybe a change in subject would be good. She had questions that needed answers, and as he was the only one she knew who could answer them, avoiding him was no longer the best strategy. As a matter of fact, spending more time with him would be necessary.

Ryanne ignored the flutter in her stomach at the thought. "Duncan?"

He stopped humming. Glanced at her out of the corner of his eye. She thought she saw a flicker of unease, and he gave her a wary, "Aye?"

Deciding that being blunt about what she needed to know would be the fastest way to get answers, she asked, "Why is the self-appointed prince o' Faeries hanging around with a pack of werewolves? And how long has this been going on?"

At her question, his big body relaxed. He shifted into a more comfortable position. "Tae be honest, I dinna ken th' why o' it. No' exactly. Except he says we need tae band together tae stop th' ones who were trapped in Faerie land during th' last war. Th' portal is no' holding. And th' soul suckers will be set free soon tae wreak havoc upon humans, Fae and shifters alike."

That was strange. Her father should be the last one who would want to prevent that from happening.

"Why do ye want tae kill yer father?" he asked in a low voice. "Kill yer blood?"

Because he deserved it. And she, as his daughter, was the only one who would be able to do it. "Doesn't he want to do the same to me?"

"Aye. But he's thousands o' years old and completely off his head. No' that that's an excuse," he was quick to add. "I dinna ken how he could want tae harm ye, either, but I can almost understand how he would think it. But ye...yer no' daft. Ye appear tae be perfectly right in th' head, so ye must have some pretty big reasons tae risk yerself this way tae come after him. Ye must have yer reasons tae want tae kill th' male who sired ye. Ye must..." His jaw snapped shut with an audible click. He sighed, his lips pressed together. "I apologize, lass. I dinna ken why I tend tae ramble on around ye."

Ryanne touched him on the arm and felt the muscles tense beneath her fingers. "My father isn't as crazy as he likes you to believe, wolf. He's actually very intelligent. And very powerful. He needs to be stopped, before it's too late. And I'm the only one who can do it."

"Why is that?"

"Because he thinks I won't. Or can't. And because I *am*

his blood." Ryanne thought about what he'd said. Perhaps she needed to meet with his pack. She could warn them, tell them what she believed was really going on.

They drove another mile or two in silence. "Where are ye stayin', lass? Where can I drop ye?"

"The same spot as before will be fine. My...rental is near there."

Eyes wide, he stared at her. "In th' woods? I ken ye dinna want anyone tae ken where yer are, but there's nothing around there for miles."

"You'd better watch the road. You're going to miss the turn." She pointed just ahead, where the hidden turnoff was rapidly approaching. "Besides, I like to walk in the woods at night. It's peaceful."

After a quick look in the rearview mirror, Duncan slowed down and crossed the grassy median, then floored it, taking them in between the trees and onto the rocky path. Ryanne held on as they bumped and jumped up the mountain, a grin on her face. Truly, he could've taken her a few more miles down the highway so she'd be closer to the cabin, but this was so much more fun. She'd never been off-roading before, and she was kind of disappointed when he pulled to a stop in the same small clearing as before.

Duncan turned off the engine. It was suddenly quiet, except for the sound of their breathing. "I wish ye would allow me tae take ye somewhere where I would ken ye are safe." Hands still on the steering wheel, he stared intensely out the windshield at something and wouldn't look at her. "Although I ken why ye dinna want tae tell me."

Again, his protectiveness touched her. She'd never had anyone show so much concern whether she made it home or not. Ryanne studied his profile. Such a handsome male. And kind. Shifter or not, she would be lucky to call him hers. And Ryanne had never had anyone to call her own. It was by her own choice, mostly. Relying on others had never played out well for her.

But this one...something told her that despite unwillingly giving her presence away, this one she could trust.

Making a decision, Ryanne took off her seatbelt. Perhaps she was being rash, but something drew her to this wolf. And she could not stand to see him sitting over there, looking so lost and alone and angry at himself.

Hiking her dress up to her thighs, she climbed over to his side. Duncan dropped his arms and pressed back against his seat as she straddled him. When he realized what she was doing, his jaw clenched tight, but he didn't try to move her away.

The steering wheel pressed into the soft flesh of her ass and her bare leg was squeezed between the seat and the door on the one side, but she knew he would never come to her. So, she would go to him.

"What are ye doin', Ryanne?"

Gods, she loved the way her name sounded coming from his lips. She wanted to hear him say it while in the throes of passion. "I want to kiss you again."

He shook his head. "This is no' a good—"

She pressed her fingers to his mouth, stopping his protests. "I just want to kiss you." She wanted to do more than that, but as he was stiff as a board beneath her, she would go easy on him. He wanted her. His actions up until now had made that very clear.

And the way he was acting right now made it very clear he was afraid.

Settling herself more securely in his lap, she rested her forearms on the back of his seat to either side of his head. Her face was only inches from his. And she couldn't help but think again just how handsome he was. "Just a kiss, wolf."

"Lass, why must ye torture me like this?" The words were little more than a whisper of anguish.

"Tell me you don't want this, and I'll get out of this car and go on about my way."

"It's no' a car. It's a Jeep, and her name is Vina."

She blinked at him, barely suppressing a smile. "That's your argument?"

He stared at her, his eyes roaming over her features like a male starved, and the pain that filled them tore her heart apart. "I…" He swallowed and tried again. "I…I…I do want tae kiss ye, lass. But, I—"

She shook her head, cutting him off. "No 'buts'." Before he could say anymore, or try to talk her out of it again, she leaned in.

The kiss was but a whisper in the dark. A secret between the two of them. Barely a taste. And it shot through her like a bolt of electricity.

Her wolf groaned low in his throat, a sound of need and frustration. "I can no'," he told her. "Ryanne…"

Her name was a sob, torn from him like she had reached in and yanked out his heart with her bare hand. "Touch me, Duncan. It's okay," she whispered against his mouth when he shook his head. She increased the pressure on his mouth, licking the seam of his lips. "Touch me," she repeated. With a nip on his bottom lip, she kissed her way across his jaw to his ear. "Touch me." She bit his earlobe. "I want to feel your hands on me, Duncan. I want them everywhere. Please," she begged. Gods, how she wanted his hands on her. Ryanne hadn't realized just how much until this very moment.

He was breathing hard, his chest rising and falling beneath her. But as she made her way back to his mouth, she felt his jaw tremble beneath her lips.

Ryanne paused. He wasn't fighting her. Quite the opposite. Every sound he made encouraged her to continue exactly what she was doing. So no, he wasn't fighting her. But he was fighting himself. And since he wouldn't tell her why, she was just going to have to help him win the right side of the battle. "Touch me," she said again. "It's okay."

As her lips moved over his, she spread her legs wider, pressing her core against him. Through the thin material of her underwear, she felt the hard seam of his jeans and rubbed against it. It felt good. But not as good as he would feel against her.

Or inside of her.

He gasped into her mouth, and then, with a growl unlike anything she'd ever heard, his hands rose from the seat. They hovered in midair, inches from her legs, until, like magnets to steel, they slammed against her body. For a moment, she was afraid he was going to throw her off of him, but then she the material tighten as his hands fisted in the skirt of her dress before spreading wide again, his fingertips digging into the soft flesh just above her thighs. He kissed her so hard she knew her lips would be bruised the next day.

Tugging at her skirt, he lifted it higher, sliding his hands beneath the loose material to her bare flesh beneath. Pulse pounding through her veins, Ryanne broke off the kiss and lifted up onto her knees so he could get it past the steering wheel. Then she felt the rough warmth of his palms on her thighs and hips and ass, pulling her close again. Hot and urgent, he branded her skin everywhere he touched.

Desire shot through her as he bucked up off the seat, meeting her halfway and crashing his hips against her. She kissed him again, unable to get enough of his mouth on hers, hanging on to his shoulders as the kiss turned into something primitive. Desperate. Filled with a need so hot and tormented she wanted to rip his clothes from him and join them together right then so he would know he wasn't alone anymore.

Ryanne vowed to herself, right then, that this male would never be without her. She didn't know what would happen between them after this night, or how they would both feel. But she knew he was in pain. Knew he felt lost and alone. Much like she did. And they needed each other.

With a harsh sound, he jerked his face to the side, then just as quickly wrapped his arms around her and pulled her against his body, hanging onto her like she was the only stable thing in the storm raging within the interior of the Jeep.

Ryanne put her arms around his neck and hung on tight. She didn't know what it was about him, but she felt his pain as if it were her own. Felt the same desperate need to be with him. Desire pulsed throughout her body even now—her nipples hard and sensitive, her core wet and ready to receive him.

She kissed his cheek, the side of his throat. "I'm aching for you," she told him honestly.

He blew out a breath, fast and harsh. As though he couldn't help himself, one hand wandered down over her hip, fingers skimming over her bare thigh toward her core.

"Yes," she encouraged him. "Touch me. Touch me there. Feel how wet I am for you."

"I want tae," he whispered. His hand slid between their bodies, finding the exact spot she needed him. He growled deep as he felt between her folds and his fingers became slick with her arousal.

His big body shuddered beneath her.

Ryanne's head fell back as he explored. Finding her entrance with two fingers, he pushed his way inside. Her muscles tightened around him, eliciting another low growl.

Withdrawing them slowly, she moaned as he put his fingers into his mouth and sucked, tasting her. Ryanne watched as he licked them clean like she was the best thing to ever hit his tongue, his glowing eyes drilling into hers as he did so until she was unable to look away.

Ryanne couldn't wait anymore. She wanted him inside

of her. And she wanted him right now. Reaching between them, she found the fastening of his jeans and tore it open with shaking fingers.

Duncan suddenly stiffened beneath her. Fast as a striking snake his hand grabbed her wrist and pulled it away. He looked away, his eyes shut tight and his features twisted in pain.

At first, she thought she'd hurt him. A male's reproductive organs could be very sensitive.

But no, that wasn't it, was it?

Eyes still closed, as though he could hide the whirlwind of emotions raging through him, he whispered, "Lass, I can no'."

Ryanne stilled.

Oh.

Oh.

This is what he'd been trying to tell her. And she'd been stupid not to listen to him. She'd put him in this position, forcing him to admit something to her he obviously wasn't comfortable sharing. *She* was the one causing him this pain. "What happened to you?" The words came out before she could hold them back. But now that the question was asked, she truly wanted to know.

"I dinna want tae speak o' it tae ye." He opened his eyes, but wouldn't look at her, instead turning his head to stare at the window, fogged over from the rain and their heavy breathing. Blood rose to the surface, coloring his neck and cheeks, but he held his chin high. "It's no' something I can... I dinna...it was during th' war..."

Oh, my gods. "Shhh. You don't have to tell me." And he didn't. Ryanne knew what her people were capable of. The question was, had they physically deformed him? Or just mentally? Sometimes the second option was more fun for them. And if that was the case, then there was hope that it could be overcome. "Duncan?"

"Aye," he answered, but he was gone. He wasn't with her anymore. Even though he was right there.

"May I still touch you?"

A shuddering breath went through him.

"Please?"

"Why would ye want tae do that when ye ken it will no' work?"

Ah. If she was reading his response correctly, his battle scars were mental. That was good. And bad. "I just want to feel you. To be close to you as you've been to me." She wouldn't force things anymore. It was important he didn't feel any more anxious than he already did.

His fingers dug into the sides of her hips, but he gave her a quick nod of consent.

Ryanne kissed his cheek, feeling the heat of his shame beneath her lips. It only made her more determined. This kind, beautiful male had nothing to feel ashamed about. Nothing at all.

Making her way to his lips, she kissed him until he responded. Until he was moaning with need. Need that she now knew was for an act of intimacy he believed was completely out of his reach. Ryanne slid her hands beneath his shirt. Warm skin over hard ridges of muscle that tightened everywhere she touched. Higher, she found the soft hair in the center of his chest. Just enough to feel masculine. She ran her fingers through the soft curls, wishing she could feel the softness of them against her bare breasts. Edging upward to his shoulders, she took his shirt with her, lifting it up and over his head.

Duncan groaned when their lips parted but lifted his arms so she could pull it off.

Ryanne leaned back, her appreciative gaze touching everywhere her hands had been.

Beautiful wasn't the word to describe him.

Duncan was masculine perfection. Thick shoulders. Muscular biceps and forearms. Flat stomach. Not an ounce of extra flesh. Hard and powerful. The kind of male who could protect you from any threat.

The ache of desire low in her belly that had never completely gone away flared to life. "You're beautiful," she told him as she ran her hands over his powerful shoulders and biceps, only to return to his chest and slide down his abdomen. "Perfect. Like the gods created you just for me."

"Maybe at one time, lass. But no' now."

He moaned when her lips returned to his throat. Kissing. Biting. Everywhere she could reach. He tasted slightly salty, like the breeze by the ocean. But richer, and with a hint of the feral creature he was.

When her hands returned to the fastening of his pants, he stiffened. But Ryanne murmured words of reassurance, telling him of her need to be close to him. To touch him. To feel him against her.

Unable to deny her, his hands fell to her thighs, where they rested as she worked. Opening his jeans, Ryanne urged him to lift off the seat and shoved them as far down as she could.

A sound caught in his throat when she found him. Silken skin that slid easily over a solid core. He was a good size, even as he was. And her legs went a bit weak imagining how glorious he would be when fully aroused.

Ryanne didn't rush him, returning her lips to his as she let her fingertips roam gently over him. When his fingers dug into her thighs, she reached beneath her hair and undid the few buttons at the back of her neck. Pulling her new dress up and off, she dropped it into the passenger seat.

CHAPTER 11

Duncan watched her bonnie dress float down to land in a soft pile of blue flowers on the passenger seat. Ever so slowly, he moved his eyes over to Ryanne to see what had been revealed.

His eyesight wasn't as good in the dark when he was in his skin, and Duncan felt a swell of sorrow rise within him when he couldn't see her as clearly as he would've liked. But it never had a chance to break the surface. For as though the gods knew how badly he needed this, the clouds parted and the light of the full moon shone through his window, bathing her in its glow.

A low moan escaped him. Ryanne was wearing something lacy and blue that matched her dress. A dark curl that had escaped her ponytail lay over her shoulder, the end curling around the edge of one full breast. He could even see her nipples through the thin fabric of her bra, hard nubs surrounded by darker circles of delicate skin.

Duncan swallowed hard. He tried to tell her how perfect she was, but could not find his voice.

Lifting one hand, he touched the heavy bottom of one bonnie breast with his fingertips, feeling the soft material with his fingertips, then ran one finger along the top edge. She had a few freckles that disappeared beneath the lace, but only on the left side.

He really wanted to see where those freckles led.

Ryanne reached behind her, and the bra fell loose. Slowly, she pulled it down her arms, baring her breasts to his hungry gaze, and tossed it to the side to lie on top of her dress. They hung heavy and full without the support, but to Duncan, they were even more perfect in their natural state.

Following the freckles, he traced a light blue vein to her nipple, then brushed his palm over the hardened tip. Completely transfixed, he hefted the weight in his hand and bent his head, bringing the nipple to his mouth.

It had been so very long since he had been intimate with a female, he'd nearly forgotten how wondrous it could be.

His lass moaned, arching her back to give him more. She was nearly naked now, only the thin material of her panties between them, and her boots on her feet.

Duncan had the sudden urge to feel all of her against all of him. Flesh against flesh. If only to feel a part of her in the only way he could.

But he was not expecting what happened next.

As he teased the hard buds of her breasts with his tongue and teeth, Ryanne reached between them. Automatically, he tensed. He didn't want her to touch him there. Didn't want her to be disappointed.

But she was not touching him. Och, no.

The lass was taking her own pleasure.

Releasing her breast, he replaced his mouth with his hands, kneading the full mounds as he pushed her gently back against the steering wheel so he could watch.

Her hand was down the front of her panties, and it was moving. Duncan could imagine what she was doing, but it wasn't enough, he needed to see more.

With one easy tug in either direction, the thin material covering her ripped in two, falling away to either side and giving him the perfect view of the dark curls between her thighs and the moisture on her elegant fingers from the dark pink flesh of her womanhood. Flesh he'd felt with his own fingers and wanted to touch again.

Ryanne's fingers slid between her folds, and as he fondled her breasts and pinched her nipples, they moved faster and faster until her head fell back and her body arched. Moans of pleasure left her sweet lips, and she began to move, undulating against him. Flesh on flesh. Helping herself to his useless body. She braced her free hand behind her on his knee, and slid her wet heat over his cock.

Watching her, his breath came in short bursts and his heart beat fast and hard in his chest. Gods, he'd never seen a more erotic sight in his life. And he'd lived a good long time.

So caught up was he in the erotic sight of her gyrating on him, it took him a moment to notice that something was happening. Something he never would've thought *could* happen. Something miraculous.

He was getting hard.

And not only that. He was feeling...things. Things he hadn't felt in a long, long time and never thought he'd feel again.

Ah gods, he'd forgotten the hunger. The wanting. The craving. Until his blood was rushing hot through his veins and his entire body ached with need and his cock swelled until it felt like he was about to burst from his skin if he didn't get inside of her. The air rushed in and out of his lungs, hot and harsh. "Ryanne!" Her name was a hoarse cry that burst from him uncontrollably.

Grabbing her hips, he lifted her. Curls falling into her face, she braced her hands on his shoulders as he lined himself up with her entrance and pulled her down hard on his cock.

He slid inside fast and rough, terrified if he didn't it would be too late. That the feelings would stop. Her body was tight and wet and hot around him, squeezing him with a sweet agony as her cry of surprise mixed with his.

Both amazed and terrified, Duncan realized he was trembling from head to toe. But he couldn't help it or hope to stop the tremors. Tears filled his eyes and he squeezed them closed, not wanting her to see his weakness, but they leaked over to wet his cheeks anyway. Still, he didn't stop. Blinking rapidly to clear his vision, he watched their joined bodies, watched as his lass moved over him, his hands on her hips guiding her, faster and faster.

Such were his emotions, his wolf prowled just below the surface as things began to tighten inside of him, tearing at his skin from the inside. With a growl, Duncan forced it into submission. He would not have this moment ruined by his own damnable nature.

Ryanne moaned his name, and her hand returned to the soft curls between her bonnie thighs as she whispered sweet things. Needy things. Dirty things. Urging him on.

Gnashing his teeth together, he tried to hold on. Just a bit longer. Dammit, just a little bit longer! He didn't want this to end. Not ever.

Dragging his eyes from her pussy, they wandered up over her soft belly to her breasts. They were a thing of pure beauty, bouncing with every thrust.

Duncan couldn't tear his eyes away.

Was this a dream?

More tears leaked out.

Please, dinna be a dream. Please!

He never thought he'd know a female like this ever again. Thought he was no more than a eunuch. He had tried. He had tried for months afterward with human and supernatural women alike, only to slink off with his tail between his legs and a hole of loneliness in his chest so deep he thought for sure someday he would concave into it and be lost. He'd even tried with nothing but his own hand. Tried until his skin was raw and sore and he'd sat on the floor of his shower, sobs wracking through him when he realized he would never be the same again.

Eventually, he'd gotten bits of himself back, and learned

there were other ways to make a female feel good. A kind word. A gentle touch. A compliment. A wink and a smile.

A dance, where they could both pretend to be more than they were, if just for a few hours.

It was all he could give them. And he had convinced himself it would be enough. But, now…

Now…

Waves of heat rolled through him, and he realized his lips were moving and he was saying things. Words of adoration and gratitude. Begging her not to stop.

Suddenly, his Ryanne cried out and her body contracted around him as she came.

That was the moment he lost it.

Worried he would hurt her but unable to stop himself, his hips jacked up as he pulled her down to meet him. Duncan slammed into her, faster and harder, as the tears rolled down his face and harsh sobs tore from his throat. His heart pounded in his chest till he thought it would explode. And those feelings…

Och, those feelings…

He cried out as a pleasure so intense it was painful slid down his spine and tightened his balls. His orgasm slammed through him, and Duncan's head smashed back into the headrest, his thigh muscles screaming as he tried to push even deeper inside of her tight body. He never wanted to have to leave her. Her name tore from his throat, and Duncan lost himself completely in the arms of the female who had brought him back to himself. Who had loved him whole again.

When he had given her all he had, and only little tingles remained, he collapsed into the seat with Ryanne's luscious body wrapped around him. He couldn't move. Couldn't speak. Could barely breath. Later, he would swear he'd gone to his death for those long moments, only to come back to life when he'd felt her lips on his throat.

Duncan held her close, feeling as though his heart were about to burst with gratitude and oh, so many other things. Emotions he had no name for and couldn't possibly contain in one body. Surely, they were about to burst from him, splitting through his skin and breaking his bones much like his wolf. Only this time, with such force, he didn't know if he'd ever be able to mend together again.

Ryanne stirred, and he only realized he was still crying when he felt the cold air hit the wet skin of his chest. He sniffed and raised his eyes from her bonnie breasts to apologize. Not for his tears that he could not contain, but for wetting her with them.

He found her staring at him with a sweet smile on her wee face, and Duncan's apology turned to acid on his tongue.

His Ryanne's warm, brown eyes were glowing with color. Pinks and blues and yellows and greens.

Only one tribe of Fae had eyes that changed to rainbows when their emotions were high. The *an olc.*

Only one tribe had the ability to play such sick games of war they could render a strong, virile male into something weak and impotent.

The same Fae who had captured him during the war.

Tortured him. Fucked with his head and his body until he was something other. Something less than a male.

Before he could check himself, he bared his canines at her with a snarl and lifted her off his lap and back into her seat. He barely contained the urge to throw her through the window. But something stopped him at the last minute. Wrenching the door open, he stumbled out into the rain with his unfastened jeans barely covering his bare ass.

Logically, he knew he was acting purely on his instinct to survive. The odds were slim to none Ryanne was one of the Faeries who had nearly driven him mad for months until Cedric had found him and taken him out of that hell. By all standards a broken shell of a male.

Cedric had saved him. Body and soul. And for that, he would be forever in debt to the alpha and would never do anything to betray him.

But logic wasn't doing him much good at the moment.

"Duncan? What's wrong?"

Ryanne came into his line of vision, covered again and looking bonnie in her dress with the blue flowers. Only the mess of her ponytail and the colors still swirling in her eyes evidence of what they'd just done.

A growl rumbled in his chest. His wolf, trying to protect him. Or maybe trying to protect her. Duncan couldn't tell.

He feared he would never be able to look upon little, blue flowers again without going mad. "Stay away from me," he told her.

"Duncan, it's—"

She came toward him, her boots squishing in the mud.

Rain began to fall, splattering off her hair and skin, and he held up a hand to stop her before she could touch him. It was funny, the things one heard when they were on the brink of losing their mind.

And their manhood.

Screams echoed in his head. His own and his wolf's. Had she ever heard a wolf scream in pain?

Had she been there?

Did it matter?

She was one of them. Nothing would ever change that. Even if she was kind now, she would change. Just like all the others. Just like Marc's Bronaugh. The dark Fae magic would be too much for her to contain or control, and eventually, it would overtake her until she became something evil and un-pure. Her heart and mind would deteriorate, and in her quest to fill the void, she would become addicted to souls. Feeding like a mindless parasite. Mad from the hunger.

"Duncan, you're shaking. Please talk to me."

But he couldn't talk to her. He couldn't even see her. All he saw were those eyes. Those fucking pinwheels of hell. He couldn't let her drag him back there. Not again. He would rather she just cut off his cock and be done with it then put him through those horrors again.

With fumbling fingers, he tried to fasten his pants. To hide himself. And then suddenly, he stilled. Was that what this had been? Was this only a trick of the Fae? His chin dropped as he stared at his flaccid cock lying limply to the side. Had any of that been real?

Those emotions he'd felt, the ones that were beginning to make him feel like a true male again, began to slowly bleed out of him. He could practically see them drain from his pores and down his body, gathering into rivers to join the rainwater running through the muck on the ground.

Duncan heard a horrible sound, long and drawn out, and it took him a moment to realize it was him. He pressed his palms to either side of his head. "Stop!" he roared. "Stop!"

"I'm not doing anything!" she cried, taking a step toward him. "Duncan, please."

His skin slid and shifted over his muscles, and he bared his canines. "Haud yer wheesht!" he cried. He didn't want to hear what she had to say. It was all a trick. "Ye stay away from me, ye devil. Or ye will no' like wha' happens."

It was a bluff. If she pulled out her magics, he would be able to do nothing but melt into a puddle of fear at her booted feet. Her boots. Boots. The prince always wore boots, and something pulled at his thoughts. Something important he should be paying attention to. But he couldn't focus on it enough to figure out what it was.

Ryanne stopped where she was but didn't leave as he'd asked. "Duncan." She spoke in calm even tones. "Please tell me what I did. Tell me what's happening."

What she did? He didn't know. Had she done anything?

Had she been there?

Had she laughed at him with the others?

Was she laughing at him now?

She came closer, walking slowly, hands out in front of her.

Bracing his feet in the mud, he jacked forward at the waist, threw his arms up and screamed. Screamed right into her bonnie face. "Get away! Get away! Get away! Dinna touch me!"

With a loud sob, she shut her eyes and disappeared right before his very eyes.

Duncan stilled, listening. But he could hear nothing above the sound of the pulse in his ears. He inhaled, trying to get his bearings.

Where was she?

Flowers. Flowers everywhere.

His hands shook so hard he finally gave up fastening his jeans and left the button undone. He whipped around at every noise, real or otherwise, searching the forest around him. But it wasn't the dark, mountain forest of his home he saw.

Instead, it was the moss-covered stone interior of a cave deep within the northern mountains, lit by a rainbow of colors from the glowing eyes of the *an olc*. In his ears, he no longer heard the whisper of the trees or the pattering of the rain. No. He heard the grunts and screeches of the soul suckers as they fought within their cages. The rain became the rush of a waterfall. And in his ears, the calm voices of his captors whispered in a language he didn't understand as they sent him to the deepest depths of a masochistic hell with nothing but words and magic.

The growls of creatures he couldn't see but could only sense came at him from every direction. Duncan spun around, arms flailing at things that weren't there, his eyes wide and unseeing, burning from his tears.

"Get away from me!" he roared.

His wolf paced beneath his skin, wanting to escape, but even that great beast was held captive by a terror so overwhelming it could not force its way out. A familiar feeling of helplessness washed over Duncan.

More growls.

Footsteps all around him.

No. No! They would not take him. Not this time! "Stay th' fook away!" he screamed. His knees gave out and he dropped to his haunches, arms coming up to protect his head even though he knew it would do no good. The things that were coming weren't something he could hit or bite or claw. They held him down with unseen hands and bared him for all to see while they whispered sick scenarios in his ears. Starved him and kept him from sleep until he believed those things were actually happening to him.

Even though Cedric swore to him no one had touched him. Told him he was a whole man yet. Stood him in front of a mirror and made him look, made him see there was no blood, no missing parts, no physical pain, nothing that wasn't always as it was.

Except his mind.

But Cedric had been wrong. Even after the horrors had faded and he no longer woke screaming in the night, he'd never again been a fully functional male.

And now they were back. They'd sent Ryanne, a lass he wouldn't be able to resist. Sent her to fuck with him some more. To make him believe his lonely existence was finally over.

She was here, somewhere. He could still sense her. And the others were with her now.

They were coming for him.

A keening cry tore from his throat just before he was hit from the side and knocked into the mud.

CHAPTER 12

R yanne heard Duncan scream into the rainy night. She was a good mile away, yet still, she heard him. The pain and fear in that scream cutting through her like shards of glass.

She had no idea what she'd done to bring about this change in him. And as she wiped the rain drops from her face—or were those tears?—she considered going back and trying one more time to talk him out of whatever black pit of suffering he was sinking into.

Walking in circles, she chewed on her thumbnail and tried to figure out what to do. Give him some space? Go back and make sure he was all right? Disappear from his life forever?

A sharp pain cut through the center of her chest until she could barely catch her breath.

One thing she did know—she'd never been loved like

that wolf had loved her. All he'd needed was a little encouragement, and she was so glad she hadn't given up on him.

At least, until he'd taken one look at her afterward and lost his mind. She'd done nothing but smile at him.

He'd stared at her like he'd seen a ghost.

He'd stared right into her eyes...

Ryanne came to an abrupt halt.

Oh, gods.

Her eyes. It was her eyes.

He didn't know what she was. He'd assumed she was *na maithe*, a faerie of the light and happy variety, so to speak.

Well, at least until now.

But how could he not have known? His pack was scheming with her father. If he knew what her father was, then he should have known what she was.

And then she had a very chilling thought.

Could it be they didn't know about the so-called prince?

A horrific scream echoed through the trees.

Ryanne took off running as fast as she could go. She was nearly back to her wolf when she heard them. Footsteps that weren't her own.

Immediately, she made herself unseen again as a wave of fear crashed over her. Not her fear. Duncan's. She froze where she was and listened, shivering from the damp, night air that suddenly seemed so much colder.

The rain dripped through the trees. An owl hooted somewhere close by, pleased with its kill.

There. More footsteps. One sounded like a human. The others...did not.

Wolves?

Dammit. Thomas's wolves were still here. Still searching for her. It had to be. If going back to the club hadn't been stupid enough, coming back here most definitely had been. They were lucky they hadn't been intruded upon a few minutes earlier. Both she and Duncan could've been slaughtered, and she doubted either of them would've noticed.

A bellow of rage echoed through the trees.

Duncan!

Ryanne ran forward a few steps without thinking. Stopped. And then, with a shake of her wet hair, continued on. Her wolf was hurting and vulnerable. If the others had taken him unawares, he would be killed without a doubt.

She had to help him.

"Dammit, Thomas!" Keeping her voice down, she cursed him all the way back to the Jeep. Still a good distance away, she took to the trees to avoid being heard or scented, and jumping from branch to branch, circled around until she could see what was happening.

Duncan was flat on his back in the mud, arms and legs akimbo like he was sacrificing himself to the gods. Two large wolves, both in various shades of brown, circled around him. A male in his skin stood off to the side in a dark raincoat, arms crossed over his chest as he stared down at Duncan. He was frowning.

After a moment, he flicked his hand like he was waving away a bug. "Get rid o' him. He will no' be telling us anything like this."

In a surge of panic, she jumped down from the branch

she'd been sitting on and rushed toward them. "Hey!" she yelled.

The two wolves spotted her immediately, dropping their heads and baring their teeth. It was a stroke of bad design that they had the ability to see her when she didn't want to be seen.

The one in his skin dropped his arms back down to his sides, his eyes scanning the trees where she stood.

"I'm the one you're looking for," she said as she strode forward. Flicking a brief glance down at Duncan, she saw blood trickling down his temple. Just out of pouncing distance, she stood with her feet braced and her arms at her sides, ready to move quick if the need arose. She tilted her head at the leader. She hadn't seen this one before. Must be new.

Which meant he had no idea who he was dealing with.

"Come on, dogs. Come and get me," she taunted. And just so their leader wouldn't miss out on all the fun, she made herself visible again.

There was a movement in the mud as Duncan's head slowly fell to the side. She felt, more than saw, his green eyes lock onto her.

The two wolves paced restlessly from side to side, heads down and tails straight out.

"What are you waiting for?" she taunted. But they were smart not to charge her. She could take at least one of them out before the other one got its teeth in her, and it appeared neither of them wanted to be the dead one.

Of course, if the leader shifted, she'd be in a world of

trouble. Even a Faerie of Ryanne's caliber couldn't take on three wolves at one time.

The smaller one was getting restless. Ryanne could tell from the way he kept sending their leader little growls and looks from the corner of his eye. He was a dominant wolf, despite his size. Nearly as dominant as the one in charge, and he obviously didn't like being told what to do.

Ah, a rebellious one. He was going to break protocol.

Ryanne smiled. This is what she'd been waiting for. She just needed to lead them away from Duncan. And with any luck, if she didn't make it back, his pack would come looking for him.

"If I were you, I'd tuck my tail between my legs and go back to Thomas and tell him you couldn't find me."

"Why would I do that?"

"Because he's lying to you. Just like the prince is lying to you. Killing me isn't going to do anything but take out the only Faerie who is on your side."

He went quiet, his expression thoughtful. Could it be something she'd said had struck a chord? Or was she hoping for something that wasn't there.

Without warning, the rogue wolf charged her, his companion on his heels.

"Stop!" their leader shouted, but he may as well have been yelling at the rain.

Ryanne raised her hand, extending her fingers toward the closest wolf. Blue electricity flew from the tips, striking the wolf like lightening, knocking him off his paws and holding him a foot off the ground. His body torqued in the air.

The other wolf rushed past his friend at a dead run.

She had about two tenths of a second before he got to her, and if that happened, she'd might never get out of here alive.

In a flash, she dropped the first wolf and reappeared behind them, between the two wolves and Duncan. Bad move, she realized, when she heard the popping sound of bones breaking and re-knitting and the wet, slushy tearing of muscle.

The leader, who hadn't moved from his spot beside her wolf, was shifting behind her. And the wolf still on its feet in front of her had just spun around on its back legs and was heading back her way.

Ryanne quickly weighed her options. She couldn't stay there and fight. The odds were very good one would take her down while she dealt with the other one. And she wouldn't be able to get close enough to make direct contact with their skulls that she'd be able to take them out instantly.

If she ran, she would be leaving Duncan exposed and helpless. They weren't focused on him now, but if she ran away, one or the other could very well take his frustration out on him.

And those options didn't even include the fact that the first wolf she'd zapped was already moving on the muddy ground, trying to get his paws beneath him.

She shouldn't have come back here. If she died, no one would be left to take care of her father.

No one else knew what she knew.

With no other choice, Ryanne ran. Her wet skirt stuck to her legs and her boots slid in the moss and mud, impeding her progress. And these wolves were fast. She could hear them right behind her, their footing much better on the wet ground than hers. Why hadn't she thought to pull off these damn boots before confronting them?

Panic tried to make its way into her heart, but she pushed it aside. She had no time for such nonsense. Not if she wanted them both to live.

CHAPTER 13

Duncan stared in the direction Ryanne had just run, three angry wolves on her tail. The cold mud seeped through his clothes and his head was pounding from the hit he'd just taken.

A hit that had actually "knocked some sense into him", pulling him from the terror he'd been drowning in.

She had come back to help him. Or had she come to finish him off? Lying in the mud in a stupor—bloody, beaten, and confused—Duncan blinked the rain out of his eyes and stared off through the trees.

His wolf was not bewildered in the least. It chewed and clawed at his insides, demanding to be released. And this time, it was not taking no as an answer.

Duncan yelped as muscle ripped and every bone in his body began to break and reknit itself. His spine arched off the ground, his torso twisting, reshaping into his wolf. The change was fast and hard.

His wolf had had enough. It was taking over. It needed to protect Duncan. And, even more importantly, the female it recognized as its mate.

No more sound escaped his lips as he finished shifting. And when it was done, he shook the mud from his fur, then threw back his head and howled. With his wolf fronting both physically and mentally, he was able to throw off the last vestiges of the hell he'd been trapped in. Every instinct awake and alert.

I'm coming, lass.

Head down, he took off in the direction he'd seen the wolves run. It was hard to stay on the trail with the rain coming down harder as it was, and he lost their scent more than once. Yet, somehow, he knew which way to go, more by instinct than anything else. And within a few minutes, he caught sight of the wolf trailing Ryanne and the other two.

His large paws landed silently on the wet leaves and moss as Duncan pushed himself to go faster. When he was close enough not to lose sight of the other wolf, he veered off to the side, circling around until he was running parallel.

Intent on his prey, the other wolf didn't notice him there until it was too late.

Pushing off his back legs, Duncan leapt over a tall fern and landed on the wolf's back. He clamped his jaws around the back of its neck, holding on as the force of his hit threw them both to the side.

Duncan landed on his back with the other wolf on top of him, knocking the air from his lungs, but Duncan only sank his teeth in deeper.

The wolf pawed at the air and twisted his spine back and forth, attempting to break his hold. With a deep growl, he finally managed to loosen Duncan's grip enough that he was able to scramble onto his feet. Duncan quickly followed suit.

They faced off, side-stepping in a slow circle. Heads down. Teeth bared. Yellow eyes locked with green. The other wolf feinted, then stepped back again, looking for an opening.

Calm and cool, Duncan studied the other wolf, learning his moves, his habits, his vulnerabilities. And when the chance came, he took it.

Both wolves reared up on their hind legs, coming together in a crash of teeth and claws. Growls rent the air, and the scent of blood joined the musky smell of wet fur and earth as they came together again and again until, finally, Duncan got a good grip on the other wolf's shoulder and threw him to the ground.

He stood over the wolf, teeth bared in an angry snarl and blood dripping from his muzzle. Duncan waited for the other wolf to submit to his dominance. If he didn't, he would have to kill him, and he really didn't want to do that. No, he wanted this one to live so he could run back to Thomas and tell him he failed.

The other wolf stared up at him from where he lay on his side in the mud. He held his head off the wet ground and his mouth twitched with the urge to snarl back. But in the end, he let it fall, exposing his throat and closing his eyes in defeat.

The entire fight had only taken a matter of seconds. Crucial seconds when his lass was running for her life from two other wolves. Lowering his head, Duncan gave this one a warning growl. He didn't want to see him again, or the next time he would not be so generous.

Backing away slowly, he watched for any sign the wolf was going to go back on his word. When he remained lying where he was, side heaving and eyes averted, Duncan spun around and took off at a dead run.

When he found the other two, they were circling the trunk of a large oak tree. Ryanne sat on a branch above them, soaking wet and shivering...and shouting obscenities.

What the hell was she doing?

Duncan immediately caught the scent of her blood. Cold air hit his skin as his fur bristled in outrage. The growl that rose up from deep within his chest was low and angry. How dare they harm his lass? The fact that she was safe in the tree and would heal as quickly as he could made absolutely no difference to him.

No longer two against one, the other wolves swung their heads in his direction. Ears pricked, they stared at him in challenge.

And Duncan was more than ready to take them up on it.

They charged him as one, and Duncan braced himself for the hit. The fact that he could not win this fight never crossed his mind. The moment they'd gone after Ryanne, they'd given him no choice.

The attack came from both sides at once, leaving him no room to maneuver. But he had a male's rage on his side, and he fought like a wolf possessed, taking out chunks wherever he could, the blood lust so strong, every bite only made him want more.

As the two wolves circled their prey, searching for a way to hit a vulnerable spot, Duncan stood stiff with his tail straight and his teeth bared in a snarl. His eyes followed them, knowing it was only a matter of seconds before they were on him again.

The only way this was going to end was if they killed him. And he was prepared to go out protecting his female.

"Hey!"

The two wolves whipped around toward the sound.

Ryanne stood there, looking like some sort of angry goddess risen from the sea. Her dark curls stuck to her face, her jaw was set, her feet braced apart, and her hands fisted at her sides. Blood ran down her left arm and calf, the rain washing it away as quickly as it appeared.

No, no, no, no! Go back into the tree!

Dammit! What the fook was she doing?

She looked right at him then. "I know. Wolf's honor and all that business. But I'm not just going to sit up there and watch you die, Duncan."

He growled at her in warning.

Ryanne raised one eyebrow. "Did you seriously just growl at me when I'm here to save your life?" She eyed the two wolves slowly stalking her and shrugged. "Or, you know. Maybe you could still give me a hand."

Duncan sprang forward at the same moment the first wolf went after Ryanne. By nothing but dumb luck, he'd chosen the right one. As she zapped the first one, he tackled the second one, taking it down to the ground. Jumping back up to his feet, he took a good chunk of bloody fur and muscle from its shoulder with him.

With Ryanne now in the line of fire, his purpose was renewed, and with the help of her zapping the first wolf, it gave him the time he needed.

In a flurry of snapping jaws and teeth, Duncan took out the first threat. When he turned to face the one who'd gone after Ryanne, he found it limping away, back legs dragging the ground, presumably hoping to find their leader.

As the adrenaline drained from his system in a rush, Duncan swayed and then stumbled, landing on his haunches in the mud. He was wet. And cold. And utterly exhausted, physically and emotionally. The wounds he'd sustained hit him all at once, every beat of his heart sending a pulse of agony through him.

Ryanne rushed forward and wrapped her arms around him as far as they would go to keep him from toppling over. And when he tried to scare her off, she ignored him completely. "Hush, wolf." Digging her fingers into the fur on the sides of his throat, she swung his large head around until he was forced to look into her eyes, bright with colors from the fight.

His two natures warring with each other, he tried to pull away, but she was strong, and he couldn't allow himself to hurt her.

"I'm not here to hurt you, Duncan. Let me help you." Still holding his head, she looked around. "We can't go back to

your Jeep. Not yet. And we're too far from my cabin."
Catching his eyes, she said, "Stay here. Don't move. Please."
And then she ran off into the darkness.

As soon as she was gone, Duncan's front legs gave out
and he slid down into the mud. Blood covered his fur, the
coppery smell strong in his nose. Was it his? He didn't
know, though he felt a number of good-sized wounds.
Some burned and throbbed still, others were merely a slight
sting when the rain hit them.

He kept his mind carefully blank. Or maybe he was just
too tired to think. For now, he would rest and heal, right
here in the middle of the forest. And hope another large
predator didn't sniff him out and come to investigate.

When Ryanne returned—if she returned—he would
need his strength.

His wolf snarled at the insinuation.

He didn't know how much time had passed when she
finally came back. She had a blanket folded up in her arms.
His heart leapt within his chest at the sight of her in spite of
himself.

"Can you walk?" she asked him. "Or can you shift?"

Duncan huffed out a response. No. He didn't think he
could. But he would try. For her.

It took him a few minutes to do it, and when he finally
managed, the process was long and excruciating. When it
was done, he fell to his side. His chest heaved as he desperately sucked in oxygen through his teeth.

But with the return to his skin, all of the chaos in his
mind returned. Once again, he was back in the cave, beaten

and broken. His physical wounds manifesting themselves in his head, translating into the psychological terrors he'd endured, reliving months of torture in a matter of moments.

Ryanne slapped her hand over her mouth as her eyes roved over his nude form, and when he rolled his burning eyes to her face, hers were filled with tears. She lowered herself to her knees and her hand fell into her lap. "Duncan," she whispered. Slowly, she reached out to touch him.

He jerked out of her reach, ribs screaming in pain. "Dinna touch me!"

She froze, her hand paused in mid-air. "I just wanted to see—"

"No! Dinna touch me!" Wet leaves stuck to his ass and back as he tried to put some distance between himself and his torturer. She couldn't fool him. She didn't want to help him. She was there to hurt him. To laugh at him. To make him scream until his voice was nothing but a rasp of air bursting from his lungs.

Throwing himself to the side, he managed to get his legs beneath him and then pushed himself onto all fours. She touched his shoulder and he threw up his arm, throwing off her hand, baring his teeth and snarling at her.

A sound came from her. A sound of distress that made him pause, but only for a brief second. Gathering what little strength he had, he pushed himself to his feet and staggered away.

Water hit his skin, aggravating his wounds and dripping into his eyes. He blinked fast, trying to clear his vision, but there were no colors to be seen. Only dark figures surrounding him, swaying with the breeze, their skin rough like bark to abrade his skin when he stumbled into them.

What new kind o' hell is this? What new creatures brought tae life by th' Faeries?

He had to get away. Had to get back to his pack. Where were they? Were they alive? Were they dead?

I just want tae go home.

Tears joined the rain on his face. He didn't know how long he wandered through the cold night. It could have been minutes, or it could have been hours. But eventually, he heard a wolf howl far off in the distance, and then, closer, a familiar voice.

"Duncan!"

"Cedric?" His voice cracked. He tried again. "Cedric?" His legs gave way and he fell to his knees. "Help me, Cedric. Dinna leave me. Help me." The words stumbled over each other, making no sense. But somehow, his alpha heard him.

Warm hands gripped his upper arms, pulling him to his feet, and he found himself staring into ice-blue eyes.

"I've got ye, Duncan. I've got ye."

"Dinna let them have me, Cedric. Please. Please. Dinna let them have me!"

Powerful arms wrapped around him, and he was pressed close to his alpha's hard body, the heat of his skin burning his wounds and warming his soul.

"They will no' have ye. No' ever again." The words were thick and heavy in his ear. "No' ever again."

CHAPTER 14

Ryanne ducked behind a tree and watched as a very large, very nude male with long, black hair ran up to Duncan and pulled him off the ground and into his arms.

The blanket she held fell to the mud at her feet.

A burning sensation ripped its way through her chest, immediately overridden by a wave of loss so profound she lost her breath and feared she would drown beneath it as the world spun around her.

Twisting around until she was completely hidden with her back to the tree, she squeezed her eyes shut and waited for the world to stabilize. When she peeked around again, the large male was gone. And so was Duncan.

She took a deep breath. And then another. Too late, she saw the error of her ways. Getting involved with this wolf beyond using him as an informant had been a mistake of immense proportions. Ryanne had no time to feel forlorn.

But...

It had been so long since she'd felt any kind of a real connection with anyone. So, she'd give herself these moments to feel these emotions, and then, when it was over, she would lock them down tight where they wouldn't hurt her anymore and get back to doing what she needed to do to stop her father.

A few minutes later, she took a shaky breath and stepped away from the support of the tree. The rain was finally letting up. Wringing out the skirt of her dress, she now deeply regretted her choice of clothes. For one, she was freezing. Two, although it did allow her a good range of maneuverability, the dress did nothing to protect her skin when in combat. And three, it tended to get snagged flowing out behind her when she ran through underbrush or low hanging branches.

And that wasn't even mentioning her boots. They, also, were very pretty. But were not made to run through mud and moss and leaves. They were only good for scooting around a dance floor or perhaps sitting pretty on the open tailgate of a pickup truck.

At least she hadn't wasted any money on them.

She wondered if Duncan's Jeep was still there. Maybe she should go back and check on it, instead of standing alone in the middle of the forest looking like the swamp creature.

And, maybe, if she was lucky. She'd run across something that would tell her where Thomas's wolves were hiding out. If she could get one of them alone, she could try getting some information out of *him* about her father's plans.

Exhaling another breath, a little stronger this time, she pushed the last swells of emotion down and locked them away. Later, perhaps, she would pull them out again and examine them. But for now, they were just getting in her way.

As she pulled off her boots and prepared to run barefoot back to the Jeep, Ryanne knew deep down she wasn't fooling anyone. Least of all, herself. The myriad of feelings she felt for the shifter were not something she was just going to be able to push aside and ignore. They were still there, simmering beneath the surface, creating a hodge-podge soup made up of a combination of her feelings for the wolf and her own insecurities.

A few minutes later, she cautiously entered the small clearing. The Jeep was still where they had left it. She assumed Duncan or someone from his pack would be back to get it in the morning.

Ryanne suddenly hoped it would be unlocked. If it were, it would be able to provide her a temporary shelter for the night. The fact that she could easily run back to the cabin hovered on the edge of her thoughts, and it would be the healthier thing to do, but she was reluctant to leave the memories here. Both good and bad.

As Ryanne approached the vehicle, she heard something snuffling around the other side. Thinking it was an animal, she smiled, always glad for company. But when she rounded the back bumper, it was no cute little bear cub she found nosing around, but a grown werewolf. To be exact, the one she'd zapped earlier.

Knowing she had no more than a second before he knew she was there—and thanking the gods for the direction of the winds that had kept him from scenting her before now —she raised both hands and tapped into the core of her power. Blue lights burst from her fingertips, hitting him square in the area of his heart.

It was enough to stop him where he was, but not enough to kill him. She didn't want to kill him. This was exactly the opportunity she'd hoped for, although the other wolf—the beta—would have been a better option. This one was nearly as dominant as Duncan and would be harder to crack.

Once he was on the ground, she tried the doors of the Jeep and sent up a prayer of thanks to find them still unlocked. Rummaging around, she wasn't surprised to find a thick length of chain. Anyone with an off-road vehicle should have the tools needed to pull it out of ditches and such.

Or, in this case, restrain another shifter.

Ryanne wasted no time dragging the wolf's body over to a tree and securing it to the base of the trunk. Luckily, this wolf was a bit smaller than most and it was merely a matter of flipping him onto his back and running the chain around his front legs and chest and waist, just in case he shifted when she wasn't paying attention. She had no idea how long he would be out, as she might have put a little more juice into those jolts than she'd meant to. But, hey, she'd panicked.

Once she made sure he wasn't going anywhere, Ryanne climbed into the Jeep and locked the doors to wait. In the process of searching for the chain, she'd also discovered another blanket. It was thin, but warm and dry, and she pulled it over her with a grateful sigh.

Now, she would wait.

It was almost dawn when the shifter finally stirred. He had, in fact, shifted back to his skin while he was out. But luckily, Ryanne hadn't slept, so she'd seen it happen and hurried to secure his hands and arms better.

When he woke and found himself chained to the tree, he was not at all happy. Yanking on the bindings, he tried to free himself, with no luck. And when Ryanne jumped out of the Jeep, drier and warmer than earlier if still tired, he growled at her.

"Release me, soul sucker."

She squatted down in front of him, crossed her arms over her bent knees, and grinned at him. "Is that supposed to insult me?"

He jerked at the chains. Ryanne let him do it. Rising to her feet, she stretched her arms over her head and then behind her as she tilted her head from side to side, easing the stiffness of her joints.

When he had calmed down again, she told him. "Okay, look. I know you know who I am. And we can make this easy or we can make this hard."

He glared at her, lips closed so tight they were nothing but a thin slash in his face.

"Tell me what my father's been up to. I know he's been

working with your alpha for a long time. And I need to know what his next move is."

"Why should I tell ye anything?"

"So, I can stop him."

The shifter laughed. "You will no' be able tae do that."

She sighed loudly. "Look. Tell me what I want to know, and I'll let you live. I might even release you so you can take a message back to Thomas for me."

"I dinna believe ye."

"I get that." She gave him a nod. Then brushed her hair out of her face. "That's smart of you. I wouldn't trust me, either. But really, what choice do you have?"

He clamped his mouth shut and turned his head.

Ryanne lifted an eyebrow as she regarded the male. His body was relaxed, his expression stubborn, and his attitude plain to see. He thought she was a joke.

Well, she would just have to show him the punchline. "All right, then. The hard way it is." Squatting down in front of him, she took his skull between her hands.

"What are ye doing?" he cried.

"Finding out what I need to know," she answered. "I gave you a chance, wolf. Remember that."

Blue lights shot from her fingers, worming their way into his mind. His body stiffened, and he screamed as his eyes rolled back into his head.

Thirty minutes later, the shifter was slumped at the base of the tree. He was alive, and he was awake. Kind of. Though it would probably be a while before he could speak a coherent sentence.

She'd learned her father appeared to be playing the packs against each other. Telling Thomas's pack one thing and Cedric's pack another. Thomas knew who and what her father was, and it seemed he had promised the wolf an immunity of sorts if they helped him.

And they weren't the only ones.

The prince had been very busy, ingratiating himself into the world of the Fae's biggest threat, the wolves, and making them all similar promises.

Except for Cedric's pack. That alpha was too fair and too honorable to bribe, so the prince was handling him and his pack a different way.

And the way he was taking out the threat? By mating the shifters with Faeries. Wolves would do anything for their mates. They would die for them. And, if the prince has his way, that's exactly what they'll be doing, unless they come around to see his side of things.

She wondered if he'd been in contact with the vampire covens, but they apparently had their own issues they were dealing with at the moment. That didn't mean they wouldn't be a problem for him later on. However, for now, they were a non-issue.

An engine roared and her head whipped around to the trail Duncan had used to get up the mountain. They were coming to retrieve the Jeep. Or perhaps it was Thomas looking for his missing wolves.

Either way, it was time for her to get the hell out of there.

Reaching into the Jeep, she got the blanket out and

wrapped it around her shoulders, then pulled her boots out and tucked them under her arm. She closed the door as quietly as she could and faded into the trees.

She needed a hot soak in a tub, clean clothes, and some sleep on a thick, padded mattress. But the rustic bathroom and cot at the cabin would have to do.

Maybe her little raccoon friend would come and keep her company.

CHAPTER 15

Duncan sat on the recliner in his apartment, one beer in his hand, six empty bottles on the end table near his elbow, and the television on. But if anyone had asked him what he was watching, he couldn't have told them, even though he'd been sitting there for a while now.

It had been almost a week since Cedric had found him wandering the forest in the freezing rain, half out of his mind. He and Marc had gone back the next day and gotten Duncan's Jeep. And they'd found a surprise waiting for them—one of Thomas's wolves chained to a tree, half-alive and completely incoherent. He was being held in a storage unit in an empty building the pack owned out in the middle of nowhere. No one would find him. And from what they'd told him, the male wouldn't be in any condition to scream for help for quite a while. Lucian and Brock went by every day or two and made sure he was clean and fed.

Had he done that? Chained him and left him out in the

elements like that? It was the chain from his Jeep, but he couldn't recall. He hardly remembered anything after...

After...

Tipping the bottle to his mouth, he took a long swallow. The alcohol did absolutely nothing to ease the tightness in his chest, however it still made him feel better on some subconscious level.

He'd told no one what had happened between him and Ryanne. What he thought had happened. For he didn't think he could stand to see the looks on their faces. Especially Cedric. There would be pity in the alpha's cold eyes, and Duncan wouldn't to blame him for thinking that way. Cedric had taken him out of that place all those years ago. Had sat with him for days afterward until he'd started coming back to the real world. Somehow knowing exactly what to do to support Duncan without hovering. So, no, Duncan wouldn't blame him if he didn't believe it had truly, physically, happened, and wasn't all in his head.

Hell, he didn't believe it himself. Not really.

The odds were, she had fooked with him. Probably sent here by someone to do just that. Who? He didn't know. None of the Faeries who had caught him during the war had lived through Cedric's rage.

Setting the now empty bottle down with the others, Duncan scrubbed his face with his hands. He didn't know what to think. What to believe. After Cedric had gotten him home and he'd calmed, Duncan had gotten up and studied himself in the mirror, looking for some sign it had truly happened. A scratch, a bruise, anything. But he was so busted up from his fights with Thomas's wolves he couldn't tell if any of the marks were from them or from her. A few hours later, most had healed like they'd never been there.

Now he was all wrapped up in his head. Not knowing what to believe. Too scared to trust what his instincts told him was true and too scared not to. His eyes wandered down to his lap, and he thought of taking himself in his hand for the fifteenth hundred time that day.

With a sigh, he tried to focus on the television, needing something to take his mind off of it. He'd probably never see the lass again in any case. For sure he'd frightened her off with all his ranting and raving.

A hard rap sounded on the door. Duncan turned his head, waiting for one of his brothers to come walking in, announcing themselves loudly and helping themselves to his stash of beer and snacks.

When no one entered, he frowned. Got up from the chair and started walking toward the door.

The scent of primrose hit him before he'd hit the foyer. Faint, but there.

His bare feet suddenly had a mind of their own. The closer he got, the faster he walked.

Flinging the door open so hard it would've smashed into the wall if not for the little stopper thingy, he stared at his guest with disbelief.

Ryanne stood there in jeans and a dark hoodie, the hood pulled low to hide her face. She pushed it back off her head and looked up at him, her brown eyes uncertain. "Hi," she said softly.

Was he imagining her standing there? Was this part of her Faerie tricks? For why else, in all that was holy, would she be standing in the hallway outside his apartment where anyone could find her at any second? Looking so bonnie with her curls pulled up on top of her head and her dark eyes large in her wee face?

It had to be a trick. Of his own mind or hers.

There was only one way to tell for sure. Lifting his hand, he brushed her cheek with his fingertips.

She was truly there. Standing outside his door like it was the most normal thing in the world for her to come a visiting. And even if he wasn't convinced, his wolf told him otherwise. The silly thing was turning happy circles in his gut and near howling with glee.

"What are ye doing here, lass?"

"I just wanted to check on you and make sure you were okay." She tried to smile, but it didn't quite reach her eyes. "So, are you? Okay?"

Duncan blocked the doorway, staring down at her. He blinked a few times and gave his head a shake in case his senses were scrambled, but she was still there.

The smile fell from her face. "Maybe I should just go. But, um...for what it's worth. I'm very sorry...for being me." She shrugged one shoulder. "There's nothing I can do about that, though. So..." Her eyes flicked to his and then away. "Yeah. Okay."

She lifted her hand, whether to reach out or to wave, he didn't know. Before she did either, she dropped it again and turned to leave.

If ye dinna ask her, ye will never ken.

He stepped through the doorway and out into the hall. "Wait. Ryanne, wait."

His teeth ached, his jaw was clenched so tight, and he didn't know how he would ever speak the words. But he needed to know. For his own sanity's sake, if nothing else.

On a harsh breath, he forced them out. "Was that real?" He grimaced at the tone of his voice and made an effort to calm the churning in his stomach. Terrified as he was of the answer, the task was nearly impossible. "Th' thing tha' happened between ye and me. Was that…was that real?"

She lifted her head, searching his expression.

"Please, dinna look at me," he pleaded, avoiding her eyes. "I can no' stand the pity on yer face. Just…answer th' question. Honestly, if ye will. Tha's all I ask o' ye."

In his peripheral vision, he saw her eyes drop to the open "V" of his flannel shirt. "I assume you're asking me about what happened in the Jeep. Before…um…before the wolves came."

"Aye," he whispered, so quietly he didn't know if she'd heard him, and trying not to think of the breakdown she'd graciously skirted around.

"Can I come in?" she asked. "None of the others in your pack is here right now, but that's not to say they won't come back."

Och. So distracted was he, he hadn't even thought of the others. They would scent her right away. Immediately, he stepped back and held open the door, closing it behind her when she came inside. He didn't invite her to sit down or offer her anything to eat or drink. And although the foyer was a nothing but a short hallway, she didn't take liberties and try to go in or look around.

"Duncan." Her brows came together as her eyes bounced around the small space, looking anywhere but at him. It was obvious she was trying very hard to abide by his wishes and found it hard.

As for him, he could only stare at the outlet on the wall by her left foot, tendrils of heat crawling up his neck and face. But he made himself stand there and listen to what she had to say.

"Whatever my people did to you, I am not them. And I was not there." He felt, more than saw her eyes lift to his face, and she pressed the palm of one hand against the center of his chest and one against her own. "I swear it. I was not there. As soon as the war started, I went into hiding."

On a sharp exhale, he asked, "Why?"

"Because I'd already seen what my father was doing. He was playing sides against each other, and pretending to be someone he's not, and I didn't trust him to care enough about me to respect my opinion about what he was doing. Turns out I was right."

Drawn by the conviction in her voice, he met her stare.

Her chin rose, her hand now gripping the material of her hoodie in a tight fist. "I swear it to you, Duncan. May the gods strike me down right here if I'm lying."

She fell silent, only the sound of their disconnected breathing filling the small space. He concentrated on her inhales and exhales, matching his rhythm to hers until the knots in his stomach loosened a bit.

"I know what they are capable of, especially during times of war." Reaching for his hand, she held it between both of hers. Her palms were cool and soft. "Please correct me if I'm wrong, but from your reaction when you saw my eyes, I can only imagine you were caught and tortured during the war in the vilest of ways for a male." She made a humorless sound. "A specialty of the elders in my tribe."

He said nothing. He couldn't. He could only concentrate on each breath she took. Craved each one like a lifeline, even though her very presence caused him pain. If he were able, he would laugh at the absurdity of the fates. At least he knew now this wasn't dream, or some sort of Faerie trickery.

It couldn't be, because it hurt so fookin' much.

"I wasn't there, Duncan," she repeated again. "I swear it to you on my life."

But could he believe her? Being that she was here to attempt to kill her father, the most powerful Faerie alive, he didn't know how sincere her claim was.

But that was neither here nor there. "Was it *real*, Ryanne? I need tae ken this!" The words rushed out of him.

She squeezed his hand between hers. "Yes, Duncan. It was real."

His fingers tightened on hers. A harsh sob tore from his throat before he could stop it, and he sucked in a breath, holding it in until the burning in his lungs threatened to burst them apart. He stared at the ceiling, unable to look at her wee face. By some miracle, he managed to repress vocalizing his pain. Just barely.

The tears, however…

The tears, they came. He was too full of everything to fight them.

She didn't call attention to his outburst. Instead, she kept talking, and for that he was very grateful. "There is nothing wrong with you, Duncan. You're still a virile male. What they do, it's nothing but a mind fuck. Something they're very good at, unfortunately." One of her hands released his to touch his chest. "You are a strong, virile male. And I had the soreness between my legs for days afterward to prove it."

He heard the teasing in her voice. But also the honesty. And if he were anything but a complete wreck at the moment, his chest would swell with pride.

But Duncan just didn't have it in him. Despite the warm touch of the female before him, and—now that he was paying attention—the heaviness of his balls and growing tightness of his jeans brought on by her nearness, he still couldn't help but wonder if this was nothing but another life. A mystical life that only came to him when he was unconscious. And soon he would wake up, sweating and unable to breathe, the last remnants of a scream vibrating on his lips.

"But…there have been others." He felt a right fool, carrying on like this with someone who could very well be finishing off what her people started. But who else would know the answers to his questions other than someone who knew how the Dark Fae worked? "There have been others. And I've tried. Human females. Shifter females. I've tried, and nothing...nothing happens. Nothing ever happens." He pulled his hand from hers and pressed both palms against the sides of his skull. He was making no sense at all, was he?

Ryanne took a step closer to him, and now he could feel the heat exuding from her body. Every breath he inhaled through his nose was filled with the scent of primrose. And when she spoke, he could smell the sweet citrus notes of an orange she'd eaten. "It didn't work because those women didn't know how to pull you out of your head. They didn't know what to do for you."

Something darker, muskier, filled his nose. Erotic images of Ryanne, naked and shameless and gyrating on his lap, flashed through his mind.

A low growl rumbled deep in his throat, and one corner of her mouth pulled up as her eyes flashed with colors. Duncan reached out and touched her jaw with his fingertips. The wanting of this one was an ache that went all the way to his bones.

"You didn't know, did you?" she asked softly, as her smile turned tentative. "You didn't know what I am?"

He sniffed and scrubbed away more tears with the back of his free hand in an effort to see her better. It did no good, as more only fell. But, truly, did it matter? He was not ashamed of his tears. "No, I dinna." He thought about that as his fingertips caressed her soft skin. "Or, maybe I did and just would no' admit it tae myself. I dinna ken."

She inched closer to him, and his fingers slid along her cheek to trace one wee ear. The tip was slightly pointed.

"I won't hurt you, Duncan. Although I do have to admit, I wish I'd never met you."

Her words brought about a sharp stab of pain and he dropped his hand to his side. Looking at the closed door so as not to see the disgust on her face, he winced. And then he pulled himself up. She may regret meeting him, but he couldn't say the same. "Why do ye say that, lass? For if what ye say is true, I'm *verra* glad tae have met *ye*."

"Because you distract me from what I'm here to do," she told him quietly. "Because I can't stop thinking about you ever since the day I saw you in the forest. Because I want to be near you so badly I would risk being discovered by coming inside your home. Because even now, I want to be with you, instead of planning how to stop my father. I want to help you heal. I want to reverse what my people did to you. I want to prove to you that I am not like them. And that you don't have to be scared of me, Duncan. I want..." She stumbled to a halt.

He was at a loss for words. He wanted to believe her, wanted to so fookin' badly. But she was right. He was scared of her. Well, not exactly of her. More that her being here wasn't real. What she was telling him wasn't real. That she wasn't real. That his cock was still as useless as before, and all of this was just some sort of new torture the gods had thrown upon him. And he didn't know what he'd done to deserve it.

Or worse, that she *was* real. And he was falling, arms and

legs flailing as he desperately tried to catch himself, toward a future of pain and sorrow when her own magic took her from him.

Ryanne waited, her bonnie face showing none of her thoughts. And when Duncan didn't respond, she twisted her hands in front of her and dropped her eyes. "Okay. It's definitely time for me to go." She stilled, her brow furrowed for a moment before she lifted her chin and met his gaze. "I'm sorry for what happened to you. And I won't bother you again. But please, if you take anything from this conversation, please believe that every word I've said is true."

Her hand was on the doorknob before Duncan broke out of his stupor. Wrapping his hand around her wrist, he pulled her away from the door. "No," he said. And then he frowned. He'd acted on instinct. But he did not want her to leave.

She turned to him with a question in her brown eyes. Before either one of them knew what he was doing, Duncan had her pinned to the door, a hand pressed to the metal on either side of her head, trapping her there. "No," he repeated. "Do no' go, Ryanne."

He lowered his head, capturing her mouth with his. Her lips were pliant beneath the onslaught, accepting his kiss as her body arched into him. Duncan kissed her as he'd dreamed of doing for days. Not soft. Not gentle. But with all of the hunger that had been building up inside of him this week without her.

His hands clenched into fists as he felt the blood rush to his cock, felt it swell until it was thick and hard. With a moan, he bent his knees and ground his hips against hers, trying desperately to ease the ache there. Ryanne's fingers dug into his sides, pulling him closer.

He longed to touch her. To rip the clothes from her body and take her against the door.

Instead, he broke off the kiss and took a step back.

Ryanne whimpered, her fingers catching on his flannel shirt as she tried to pull him back to her.

But he couldn't.

Not yet.

Duncan's lungs burned with the need for oxygen and he hauled in a deep breath, his eyes roaming over her face before they locked gazes.

Rainbow eyes glowed back at him. Wide and confused. "Duncan?" Her voice shook slightly.

Her lips were swollen from his kiss. Her cheeks and neck flushed. She didn't come after him, but kept her back against the door as though she knew he needed space to come to terms with the knowledge that this was the female he wanted more than life.

This was the female who called to his wolf.

This was the female who had performed a miracle.

This was the female who could, so easily, unman him once again.

"Dinna move," he told her. Then he reached out and unzipped her hoodie, exposing more skin to his ravenous gaze. Her skin was flushed, and he traced the evidence of her reaction to him until it disappeared beneath the unbuttoned neckline of a blue, thermal shirt.

This was something he had missed in the darkness of his parked Jeep. The tiny nuances, like her blood suffusing her skin with color when she was aroused. The glisten of her brow. The way her body practically vibrated with need, something he'd felt but couldn't see.

And her eyes. Those haunting eyes. They watched him closely, waiting to see what he would do. Colors rotating through them like one of those child's toys.

Duncan fought the demons in his mind. Pushed away the echoes of his own screams. It was better with the lights on. He could see her clearly, and as the memories jostled for his attention, he had only to focus on her to realize where he was and what was happening.

Ryanne. His Ryanne. Not the ones who'd hurt him.

The one who'd saved him.

His cock strained to break free of his jeans. And with a low growl, he hooked his finger on the neckline of her shirt and pulled her to him.

CHAPTER 16

Ryanne stumbled into Duncan's arms, only to be lifted from the floor and slammed against the wall, one of his large hands cradling her head and the other digging into the round cheek of her ass. The hair on the back of her head tightened on her skull as he gripped it in his fist, tugging it loose from her ponytail until curls tumbled around her shoulders. Glowing green eyes roamed her face, memorizing her features.

She wrapped her legs around his hips, waiting for him to kiss her. But he didn't.

"Are you going to kiss me again?"

"Maybe," he told her. "But right now, I just want tae look at ye."

She fought back a smile. "Okay. Are you going to do that with our clothes on or off?"

His gaze burned its way down to the opening of her

shirt and back. "Off," he decided. "Take off yer shirt, Ryanne."

Pulse racing at this new confident Duncan, she did as he told her, and it wasn't as awkward as she would've thought with him still holding her against the wall. But only because he was so damn strong. Ryanne was not the "wee lass" he seemed to think she was. She was what humans would call "plus size", with the breasts, stomach, hips, and ass of a Renaissance woman. A figure shifters appeared to prefer, however, from what she'd seen.

She was glad she'd decided to forego a bra this time, what with all the layers she was wearing and all, and as she dropped her hoodie on the floor and then pulled off her long-sleeved shirt, the possessive look on Duncan's face as he stared at her bared breasts was hotter than any sex talk she'd ever heard. And she'd heard quite a bit.

But it was the deep growl that rumbled over her bare skin that tightened the muscles in her lower belly and caused a desire to swell and surge, demanding something be done about it. Ryanne rolled her hips, arching her back, bringing her swollen nipples closer to his mouth.

Suddenly, her back was no longer against the door and they were moving. Things crashed to the floor and Ryanne was laid out on something cold and hard. Looking around, she found herself spread out across the kitchen counter like a buffet. Her boots were pulled from her feet and dropped to the floor. Her jeans and underwear quickly followed. The flow of air from the vent above cooled her heated skin as her knees were pushed apart, and soft kisses were pressed to her inner thigh. Ryanne moaned and lifted her arms above her head, giving him permission to do as he would.

It was quite obvious that this time *he* needed to be in control.

Perhaps she should insist he record a video on his phone. Then whenever he started second guessing what had happened, he could just watch the video.

The sound of his voice chased away the idea. "I've dreamed o' doing this," he rumbled between her legs. "For so verra long. Since th' first time I seen ye."

Large hands gripped her hips and she felt his tongue, warm and wet, lick between the folds of her womanhood, finding *that* spot. The one that made her forget everything but what was happening in that moment and how it was making her feel. Ryanne moaned, and tried to lift her hips to help, but he held her firm.

Every once in a while, he would emit a low growl, much like a predator did while devouring its prey.

Ryanne could do nothing but ride the waves of desire he was creating as they rose higher and higher, her entire body trembling with the need for release. Faster and faster the waves came, building upon each other until everything tightened on a surge so strong it was almost painful. Gritting her teeth to keep from crying out, she came on his tongue as he pulled her hips up off the counter so he could taste her more fully.

She was still riding out the last of it when she felt him pushing to be inside. Her muscles tightened around him, and Duncan groaned.

As he filled her, Ryanne kept her eyes closed, worried he would see how much he affected her and fall into that horrible abyss again. Afraid she wouldn't be able to pull him out this time.

Slitting her eyes open only just enough to watch him, she was oh, so very glad she had.

Her shifter loomed over her like a sculpture come to life. A fine sheen of sweat covered his olive toned skin. Every muscle sharp and defined as he moved within her, all the way down the ridges of his stomach and the slight "V" at his hips.

"Duncan." His name was a sigh on her lips as that heavy ache returned to her womb. And as he slid in and out of her body, that ache grew until she was gripping the edges of the counter above her head.

"Look at me," he growled. "I need tae see ye."

Ryanne froze, afraid, even as she shook with need.

"Ryanne." The warning in his tone was impossible to miss.

"I'm afraid," she whispered.

His movements slowed, and she felt the heavy weight of him come over her as one hand brushed tendrils of hair from her face. "Open yer eyes, lass. I want tae see ye when I come inside o' ye." With slow, lazy strokes, he kept the fire burning inside of her. "Look at me, Ryanne."

She moaned at the sound of her name leaving his lips. Slowly, she blinked her eyes open in the bright light coming from the living room.

For a horrifying moment, she thought she'd made a horrible mistake.

Duncan stopped moving as he stared at her eyes, a strange expression on his face. "This is real?" he asked her.

She nodded her head, lifting her hips to urge him on. "I feel you inside of me," she told him. "And you feel so good, Duncan. Thick and hard. So very hard." The last words ended on a moan as he began to move inside of her.

He flashed his canines with a snarl. "Ye would no' lie tae me."

"No. I would not." She started to put her arms around him but stopped. "I want to touch you."

Dropping his head, he nuzzled her neck. She took that as a yes and cradled his head to her for a moment before running her hands down his strong back as far as she could reach and back again. "I want to taste you as you did me," she confessed. "I want to take you in my mouth and give you pleasure."

His teeth sank into the muscle between her neck and shoulder and she cried out, but he only bit harder. Ryanne didn't mind the pain, and it was a minor thing if it helped him feel like he had the upper hand. "Harder," she demanded. "Fuck me harder."

Releasing her from his bite, he rose up, following her commands even as he snarled at her again.

Everything tightened inside of her, that aching fullness ascending, then diminishing, only to come back harder and sharper than before as he took her right to the edge and held her there. Ryanne arched her back, bringing him deeper with each thrust.

His hand covered her breast, pinching the swollen nipple before moving to the other one.

She was coming again, gripping his arm as his name burst from her lips. As she hovered and crashed over the edge, he swelled inside of her and with a guttural moan, he came with her, filling her...

The door crashed open.

Duncan's eyes flashed open as he pulled out of her and whipped around, baring his teeth, a menacing growl raising the hair on her arms.

Sitting up and jumping off the counter, Ryanne found his shirt and threw it on before stepping out from behind him to see who it was.

The black-haired wolf was standing just inside the apartment, icy blue eyes wide as they stared right at Duncan's cock, still wet from her and pulsing.

If Ryanne didn't know better, she would think there was something going on between the two. Between the naked hugging in the woods and now this. However, that was totally not the vibe she was getting.

Those strange eyes shifted to her, and his head cocked to the side before taking in Duncan's appearance again.

Ryanne looked between the two shifters, waiting for someone to say something. They both appeared to be in shock. So, she took it upon herself to step forward and introduce herself. As she did, her mind flew over the plans she had for her father and made some quick adjustments. "Hi," she said to the black-haired male. "I'm Ryanne."

Those eerie eyes immediately landed on her. "Yer th' prince's daughter," he said after a moment. His voice was deep. Sexy.

"Um, yes. But please don't hold that against me." She stuck her hand out further, and he finally took it.

"I'm Cedric," he told her.

Ah, the alpha. She should've known. The overwhelming presence of his aura filled the apartment until it was almost hard to breathe. "Nice to meet you."

"And ye, also." He studied her closely.

Ryanne felt so exposed beneath his disconcerting scrutiny she had to glance down to make sure she had, in fact, covered herself.

"Ryanne." Duncan called her back to him, and with a tight smile, she returned to his side. He seemed completely unconcerned with his own nakedness, as shifters usually were, standing with his arms casually at his sides. "If ye could give us a moment, Cedric?"

The alpha gave his head a little shake. "Och, aye. O' course. I apologize. I'm just…in a bit o' shock. I'll just get a beer." And then he turned on his heel and walked around the counter to the fridge.

With a hand on her lower back, Duncan told her, "Go on in tae th' bedroom. That way." He lifted his chin to indicate the right door. "I'll gather our things and be right there."

"Okay." As it appeared the alpha wasn't leaving anytime

soon, she went to the room he'd indicated to wait, closing the door softly behind her. It was a nice room, all dark gray walls and a smoky, wood floor. A few black and white paintings hung on the walls, with flecks of red accents. The bed was a king and was covered in a gray comforter only slightly lighter than the walls. There was a nightstand on either side of the bed, and a large chest of drawers at the foot, both a dark brown. An area rug done in Art Deco covered a large portion of the floor between the bed and the bath, swirled in black and white and gray with red line accents.

She took a deep breath. It smelled like Duncan in this room. Ryanne liked it very much.

On the other side of the door, she could hear the two males having a quiet conversation. Figuring she had a little time, she went into his bathroom and turned on the shower to clean up.

By the time Duncan came in, again clad in his jeans, she was sitting on the edge of his bed wrapped in a towel. His shirt was spread out beside her.

Laying her clothes down near his, he sat beside her and took her hand. "I think ye should talk tae Cedric. Tell him why yer here."

He was probably right. It was her impromptu decision to come here that had created this situation. And she would adjust. Perhaps things would work out better this way, if she could get the wolves on her side—which shouldn't be hard provided they believe her—they could assist her in her endeavors.

She didn't trust them. But strangely, she trusted Duncan.

"Yer quiet. Did I hurt ye, lass?"

The question caught her unawares. "What? Oh. No, Duncan. You didn't hurt me at all."

"Ye would no' lie tae me?"

She looked into his green eyes, somewhat surprised to find them filled with concern and a touch of fear. Fear for her. Not himself. She grinned at him, happy to know she'd taken the correct path by letting him have control. "Have I lied to you, yet?"

He searched her face for a few seconds, then brought her hand to his mouth and kissed her knuckles. "No. No, ye haven't."

"And I don't intend to start. For if I did, that would make me no better than them."

"Them?"

"My father and his minions." She released his hand and stood. "He's lying to you and your pack, and it's time you knew about it." Unwinding the large towel from her body, she dropped it on the bed and began to dress.

Duncan watched her dress in silence until she was covered, his jaw tense and his gaze hot, searing her bare skin everywhere he looked. "I feel like a right fool," he said quietly when she was done.

Ryanne paused with one shoe on and one in her hand. "For what reason?"

He kept his eyes downcast and wouldn't look at her. "For the way I acted that night."

She knew exactly what night he was speaking of. Dropping her shoe on the floor, she took his face in her hands, his incoming beard was rough on her palms, and forced him to look up at her. "You have no reason to feel shame. None at all. I only wish I could've helped you come back to me."

He met her gaze. "I'm with ye now, lass."

Her pulse picked up, and she dropped her hands, suddenly afraid. But before she could move away, he grabbed her hips, keeping her in front of him. "Ye brought me back tae myself, lass. I will forever be grateful tae ye. I will no' forget."

Why did this feel like a goodbye? She swallowed, then cleared her throat. "I'm still here, Duncan."

"Aye, I ken that. I just dinna ken what ye expect tae happen now. Between us, I mean."

"What do you want to happen?" She held her breath as she waited for his answer, not realizing how important it was to her until just this very second.

What had started as nothing more than a curious diversion with this wolf had turned into something she was not expecting. Ryanne wasn't sure how or why. Perhaps it was knowing how he'd suffered at the hands of her people. Perhaps it was how no matter his perceived physical abilities, he was male enough not to hide his vulnerability from her.

Perhaps it was that she needed him as much as he needed her.

His eyes narrowed on her face as he answered her question. "I dinna ken."

The breath she'd been holding came out on a long exhale. He was holding back. He had to be. No one loved a female like he just had without feeling something for that female. And why she even cared, she didn't know, either. But she did care, and she wasn't ready for this shifter to be out of her life. "Can I tell you something?"

"O' course. Always." Although the words were spoken casually enough, there was curiosity and a good dose of caution in his tone and posture.

A soft knock sounded on the bedroom door, and Cedric called out, "I dinna mean tae interrupt, but th' others will be back soon, and I'd like tae hear what ye have tae say, Ryanne, before yer discovered here."

Duncan opened his mouth to respond, but before he could, she answered, "We'll be right there." Then she bent to get her shoe.

"What were ye going tae say, lass?"

With a small smile, she told him, "It can wait."

The gods save her, what was she doing? Besides the fact that shifter in the other room could absolutely hear every word she said, she had no time to be getting all soft and mushy right now. Not even for a tall, good looking, vulnerable, alpha male shifter like Duncan.

She was here to stop her father. And she was the only one who had the guts to stand up to him. But it would take all of her attention. She needed to stay alert, and not be distracted. As history had shown her, her very life depended on it.

CHAPTER 17

Duncan made a note to himself to get Cedric the hell out of his apartment as soon as he was able so he and Ryanne could get back to their conversation. She'd been about to confess something important to him, he was sure of it.

Damn Cedric and his need to know things!

She didn't need to tell him what she was about to tell him, Duncan had already put the pieces together. But he wanted to hear it from her, to ease his mind.

Nonetheless, they all gathered around the kitchen counter again—only this time fully dressed and more presentable.

Cedric smacked Duncan on the shoulder when he passed by in the kitchen to get a beer for him and a water for Ryanne. Duncan frowned at the rowdy greeting, but his alpha only grinned at him, his words from earlier echoing in Duncan's head.

"Did she heal ye, then, Duncan?" Cedric had sounded equal parts thrilled and disbelieving.

"Aye," he'd told him. "Aye, I think she did."

Cedric nodded. "So, I was right all those years ago. Twas only Faerie magic messing with ye, no' anything physical."

"That's what Ryanne said. Said I only needed tae get out o' my own head. And she…uh…she managed tae do that."

Both of Cedric's hands had landed heavily on his shoulders. "I'm verra happy for ye, my brother."

Perhaps he was now, but that may change when he found out why she was here.

Duncan was pulled out of that past conversation by the one currently taking place between Cedric and Ryanne.

"I sincerely apologize, lass, for walking in on ye earlier. Ye ken I must protect my pack, and when I heard Duncan hollerin', well, I dinna ken what was happening, but I came tae check on him."

She took the glass of water Duncan handed her with a smile of thanks. "It's okay," she told Cedric. "Although I appreciate the apology." She scrutinized him for a long moment, before seeming to come to the conclusion she could trust him. "May I speak freely?"

"O' course." Cedric leaned over the counter across from her with his weight on his elbows and gave her his full attention.

As Duncan took a seat on the stool next to her, she began to speak, "I know you chose to work with my father—"

"Ha! No' my choice, believe me." Rolling his eyes, Cedric took a deep swig of his beer.

Ryanne swallowed. "He does have a way of ingratiating himself, even places he's not wanted. And Duncan tells me you also know my father thought I was dead, because he thinks he killed me."

Cedric's mouth twisted in disgust. "Aye, he did say tha'. I dinna ken who in their right mind would do such a thing tae their own bairn."

"Well, the prince is who is, and he's not as crazy as he tries to make everyone believe. He's also not the Faerie you think he is, and that's the first thing you need to know if you're going to help me."

Duncan turned to her in surprise as Cedric's eyes narrowed on her face. "What do ye mean, lass? Why would I risk my pack tae take yer side in all o' this?"

Never taking his eyes from her, Duncan told him, "She's an *olc*."

"What?" Cedric bit out the word.

He turned to his alpha. "She's a Dark Fae, Cedric. Like Bronaugh."

"Ye ken this for sure?"

From the corner of his eye, Duncan saw her look between him and Cedric. "Uh, I'm sitting right here, you two."

Duncan gave her a self-conscious smile. "Sorry, lass."

She placed her hand on his knee and gave it a squeeze, sending a shot of warmth up his thigh and right into his groin. Covering her hand with his, he held it there. He rather enjoyed the sensation, and he had a feeling he was going to be walking around like an adolescent for a while, needing nothing more than a small touch or a stiff breeze to harden him.

It was a heady feeling.

"The prince is *an olc*? A Dark Fae? Prince Nada?" Cedric voice got higher and louder with each question.

She nodded. "Yes. Why do you think he wants me dead?" Then she answered her own question. "Because I'm here to expose him, that's why."

Duncan frowned. "But he fought with us in the first war. He was on our side."

"No. He wasn't. But it all went awry, and the only way he could save himself was to pretend to be on the other side." She turned more fully toward Duncan, until her knees brushed his thigh.

Duncan shifted in his chair. He was having trouble paying attention to the conversation. All he wanted to do was get her naked again and fuck her until neither of them could move.

Then, maybe, in a week or so, take her dancing so he could hold her in his arms. They could tease each other with the soft brush of her breasts on his chest, the whisper of a thigh between hers as they stepped around the floor. The scent of her desire rising around him, making her natural primrose scent earthy and heavy.

His nostrils flared and his cock hardened.

She touched his arm, drawing his attention back to her. "Cedric, I'm not like him. I'm not like them. I tried to stop him back then, and he killed me for it. Or rather, he tried."

"What are ye sayin', lass?"

"It seems my father is playing you and your pack. Just like he played my people. He betrayed them because they disagreed with his rule. The prince is the one who *made* the soul suckers. He's the one who had the portal created to trap our people who wouldn't go along with him. And now, I believe he's trying to open it back up and release them."

"But, why would he do that?" Duncan asked. "Surely, he kens tha' if he releases th' ones he put in there in th' first place, they will no' be pleased with him."

"I think he's betting on the fact they'll be so grateful they'll follow him without question. That he only meant them to be there temporarily while he figured out a plan to remove their biggest obstacle in his plan for world domination. Namely, you."

Suddenly, Cedric's eyes narrowed in on her. "How do ye ken all this, Ryanne? If what ye say is true, ye've been good as dead all these years. So, how would ye ken what yer father is up tae?"

"I have those that have been loyal to me."

"Ye have spies?" Cedric asked her.

"Yes. But I won't risk their lives by telling you who they are."

"No, o' course not," he muttered. Pushing himself off the counter, Cedric began to pace the small space. "So, what are yer plans with th' prince?" he asked Ryanne as he walked.

"Simple. I plan to kill him."

"And how will ye do that, lass? He is th' prince o' yer people. Th' entire tribe o' Dark Fae. Tae become someone o' such importance, he would need tae be very powerful. We have seen how powerful he is. He pulls us through space and time tae wherever he needs us tae go. For sure, he pulled yer name right out o' Duncan's head! He would ken if we turned against him."

"Not necessarily," she told him. "The reason he was able to do that to Duncan was because of the level of emotion involved. My people feed off of emotion, good or bad. And, no offense, but you wolves are full of them."

Cedric nodded, then gave a self-depreciating laugh. "Aye. We shifters run hot. In all ways."

"I believe my father plans to wipe out the *na maithe* tribe, and anyone else who he can't trick or convince to allow our people free reign in this world."

A deep growl rent the air, and Duncan's upper lip lifted in a snarl. An automatic response to his alpha's distress.

"By trick, ye mean us," Cedric said.

Unaffected by his show of aggression, she lifted one eyebrow. "Why do you think your wolves are suddenly mating with Faeries?"

Both wolves fell silent at that. But then Duncan shook his head. "No. No, that is no' right. Brock's mate, Heather, is *na maithe*. They were the first tae join. Why would th' prince get them together if she's no' o' his tribe? And why wouldn't Heather ken?" He looked at Cedric and Cedric looked at him.

"Or does she ken?" Cedric asked to the room in general.

Ryanne shook her head. "She doesn't know. And she's not tricking anyone. Heather is young. As far as she's known all her life, Prince Nada is who he says he is. She has no part in this."

"She's going tae be taken out," Duncan concluded.

"Now that her job is done, most likely."

"And Bitsy. Bitsy is also *na maithe*."

"Who is Bitsy?"

"The Faerie mate of Keegan, the Texas and Colorado alpha."

"The wolf who has the Faerie rodeo?" she asked. Colors flashed in her eyes. "Yeah, that was a bad idea."

"He no longer has it," Cedric said distractedly. "So, what yer telling me, is th' prince has been mating wolves and Fae for what? Tae keep us under control?"

"Exactly," she told him. "We all know how wolves are with their mates. You would die for them."

"So, if we are mated, we will no' give him any trouble when he reveals his plans," Duncan said as Cedric nodded.

"Or so he believes," Cedric ground out. "I do no' like being taken for a fool."

"You'll help me, then?" Ryanne asked.

Cedric cocked his head and studied her. To her credit, she didn't so much as flinch under the intense stare of those cold eyes as he assessed her. "Aye," he finally said. "We will help ye, lass. What do ye need us tae do?"

Ryanne smiled. It was not a pleasant smile, and Duncan felt a shiver pass over him at the sight.

As though she felt his unease, she took his hand in hers

and held on. "That's something we will need to discuss. My original plan was to come here, find out where my father was and what he was doing, and then catch him at a weak moment and kill him. It didn't involve anyone else except to get information."

Cold fingers crept up Duncan's spine.

Memories flashed through his mind. Ryanne spotting him in the woods. Spying on him. Following him. Studying him like the specimen of a science project.

Is that what she'd been doing with him all this time? Using him for information? Is that what she'd been about to tell him before Cedric interrupted them? Again?

The devil take the lass. She'd given him back his virility only to make a fool of him.

The wall around his heart, the one she'd ripped down brick by brick with her strategic seduction, began to reform. Only this time, the bricks were thicker and stronger, the mortar holding them together near impenetrable.

Duncan felt her eyes on him, as though she could sense the turmoil inside of him, but he would not embarrass himself any more in front of his alpha.

Cedric glanced at his phone. "Th' others will be back soon. I dinna think we should tell them anything until we have a plan. And maybe no' even then. If, as ye say, Prince Nada can pull things from our heads, it might be best tae keep those things tae as few o' us as possible. Namely ye, Duncan, and myself."

Duncan nodded. "I dinna ken if even I can be trusted,

Cedric. No' right now." He didn't go into more detail. Obviously, with everything that had happened between him and Ryanne, his emotions were anything but un-chaotic.

"Aye," Cedric told him. "Ye are probably right. We'll need tae keep ye away from *his highness.*" Then he turned to Ryanne. "Can ye come back here tomorrow evening? Th' others will all be out on patrols. Duncan, I can pull ye from yer shift if ye would like."

"No. No. I'll take my shift." When Cedric looked at him in confusion, he added, "We dinna want th' rest o' the pack tae think it's anything but an ordinary night."

"Och, aye. Yer right." Cedric nodded. "So, tomorrow then?" he asked Ryanne. "At this time. We should meet here again. Yer father has a tendency tae…show up…at my place whenever he feels like it."

"I'll be here," she told him. "But we should have a back-up plan. If for any reason things change, you can find me at a little cabin not far from here, in the mountains where I first saw you, Duncan."

Surprised, he said, "Yer stayin' at Lucian's cabin? That's yer 'rental'?"

"Lucian has a cabin?" Cedric asked.

"Aye," Duncan answered distractedly. "I will show ye where it is if ye need tae go there. We should be able tae take a run in th' woods without th' others thinking much aboot it."

Cedric nodded, and stuck out his hand. "It was nice tae meet ye, lass. And again, my apologies for barging in th' way I did."

Ryanne smiled. "Not to worry. I'll see you tomorrow night. How long do I have before I need to leave?"

Cedric checked his phone again. "Say twenty minutes?"

"I'll be gone," she told him.

With a nod at Duncan, he left, closing the front door quietly behind him.

And uncomfortable silence filled the room. After a moment, Duncan got up and padded silently to the trash under the sink to throw away his beer bottle.

"Duncan, what's wrong?"

Straightening to his full height, he crossed his arms over his bare chest and turned to face her. "What were ye going tae tell me in the bedroom?"

"I don't think now's the time to get into that conversation," she said, watching him closely.

"Why no'? Because it would make things uncomfortable if ye were tae tell me ye were only using me tae get information?"

She stilled, her forehead creasing in confusion. "What? No. No, that's not what I was going to tell you."

"But it's th' truth, is it no'?"

"Duncan."

"Dinna start lying tae me now, lass. I dinna think my tender heart can take it." The sarcasm in his voice was not to be missed.

Eyes sad, Ryanne stood. "I think I should just go."

"Och, aye. Run away." He was being an ass, and he knew it fully. But if anyone had a right to act this way, it should be him. The lass had taken him for a ride, and as it turned out, he was not a fan of amusement parks.

She came to stand in front of him, and Duncan held his ground. "Come see me tonight," she told him.

"I dinna think I'll be doing that."

"You're not going to give me the chance to explain?"

"It's no' necessary," he told her. "Ye just explained everything tae me and Cedric."

"No, I did not. That wasn't everything."

"Then ye should fill in my alpha when ye see him tomorrow."

Pinks and greens and blues and yellows flashed in her eyes, but the colors were sad and subdued. Ryanne glanced away and back, then cleared her throat. "If you change your mind—"

"I will no'," he told her. "Thank ye for what ye did for me, lass. I meant what I said, and I will no' forget it. But there's no reason for ye tae hang around anymore."

To his surprise, her eyes filled with tears. But Duncan was not to be moved. He was done being a plaything for the Fae. For that's exactly what she'd done. Used his body and his mind for her own sick amusements.

Ryanne stared up at him for long moments. And then she spun away and was gone between one blink and the next.

CHAPTER 18

Duncan stood frozen for a long time. So long his spine began to ache from holding himself so stiff. When he could, he dropped his arms to his sides and exhaled.

Och, but his heart hurt. It felt as though it were burning a hole in the center of his chest. He was a fookin' *eejit* to let her get under his skin the way she had.

Though the last thing he felt like doing was going out, Duncan decided that would be the very thing. He needed to get the scent of her off of him. Needed to have another wee face in his head every time he closed his eyes. Different locks between his fingers. New curves against him and a different scent in his nose.

An hour later, showered and dressed in jeans, a light blue button-down shirt with long sleeves, and some cologne for the ladies, he stopped by his favorite steak house and ordered his favorite meal. A wink at the hostess got him a good table in the corner where he could see the exits, and when his meal came, he wasted no time emptying his plate even though his stomach was in knots.

A good stein of Scottish beer washed it all down. While he ate, Duncan watched the other patrons, even listening in on some of their conversations in an effort to keep himself out of his head. When he got the check, he left his waiter a fifty percent tip.

Thirty minutes later, he walked into the dance hall. It was a wee bit early, but the place was already filling up. Diane, a blond human lass in her early forties with an arse that filled her jeans nicely and a smile that warmed his heart caught his eye.

Duncan gave her a saucy wink and grinned.

She smiled back.

As he approached to claim her for a dance, she took a sip of her wine and fluffed her hair. Duncan had danced with her many times before, and they'd grown to have an easy partnership on the dance floor.

Even better, they'd developed a comfortable relationship off of it. Diane was a fine woman. Duncan had always wished he could offer her more than a few hours of pretending. Perhaps tonight, he would get that chance.

"Hi there," she greeted him when he arrived at her table.

"Hi yerself," he responded. When he took her hand, he kissed the back of it, ignoring the fact that every cell in his body was trying to bring this to a screeching halt before it even began.

Leading her to the dance floor, Duncan took her in his

arms. The song was a slow, lazy two-step, and as they began to move around the floor, he was glad for it. His feet couldn't seem to get it together and he kept mis stepping, starting off on the wrong foot, running into people behind him. To cover his unusual awkwardness, he told her, "Forgive me, lass. I've had a hell of a day."

"Oh, no," she said. "It's probably me. I haven't been dancing in a while and it always takes me a minute to get back into it." Diane smiled at him.

He smiled back, appreciating the way she tried to cover for him. She had a fine smile, all white teeth and crinkly eyes, and now that he thought about it, he didn't remember seeing her in quite some time. "I hope everything is okay with ye?"

"Oh, yes. Everything's fine. Just been working a lot."

He inquired as to what she did for a living, and they spent the rest of the song in easy conversation.

Yet, everywhere he looked, he saw dark curls, covert looks, and a smile that teased him with the radiance he knew was lying beneath the surface.

As they eventually fell into a more comfortable rhythm —a bit unsteady, but better then when they'd started— Duncan breathed in the woman in his arms, trying to eradicate Ryanne's scent from his being. But the perfume Diane wore, never bothersome to him before, was cloying and too strong and made him want to sneeze. A far cry from the sweet, subtle scent he'd grown used to having in his nose. One that only made him want to get closer to the soft body that wore it.

At the end of the song, Duncan stepped back and kissed her hand again. He and Diane had, at times, done a little making out before. And though, of course, it had never led to anything more, the kissing had been quite pleasant. After a brief hesitation, Duncan decided he was ready to try it again, eager to see if the response would be different now that...

Taking a deep breath to steady his sudden nerves, he said, "How aboot we get a drink?"

"Sure, that sounds great."

Keeping a hold of her hand, he led her to the bar where he ordered her another glass of wine and a beer for himself. A seat opened up on the end, closest to the back door, and Duncan took a seat, tugging Diane forward until she was standing between his legs.

They talked casually about nothing, both trying to pretend they weren't obviously aware where this was going.

When the conversation began to fizzle out, he kissed her.

Diane's soft lips tasted like the sweet wine she was drinking. They were very soft. Very pleasant.

And very wrong.

But, he persisted, pulling her in closer until she was straddling his leg in the dark corner of the bar. He heard her heart pounding over the music. Smelled the musk of her arousal. And, after a few more kisses...

It started to affect him.

Duncan fell still. Diane's hand was high on his thigh, brushing the ridge of his cock. And his cock was liking it.

But it wasn't because of the woman in his arms. It was Ryanne who filled his head. Ryanne, whose scent he craved and whose curves he imagined he was feeling against him. Whose lips he wanted beneath his. Whose moans he wanted in his ears.

With a sigh, he gently pushed Diane away. "How aboot another dance?"

Confusion flickered across her features, but she pulled herself together and smiled. "Oh, uh. Sure. Yeah."

Duncan chugged down his beer and led her out to the floor. They danced for three more songs, all more awkward then the first, before she told him she needed to go to the ladies' room and hooked up with someone else when she came out.

He wasn't hurt about it. Diane was a fine lass and she deserved to find a man who could give her his full attention.

Determined to get all thoughts of the Fae lass out of his head, Duncan threw himself into having a good time. He switched over to whiskey, danced the night away with a multitude of women, and didn't leave until they turned on the lights and kicked everyone out.

Not one of them managed to get Ryanne out of his system, though a few of the bolder ones confirmed his theory that she had been right. His lack of manliness had been all in his head, and nothing physical.

By the time he left he was feeling downright crabbit about it all.

"You reek like another woman."

She'd startled him so much he dropped his keys on the

ground, which only proved how in his head he had been. Spinning around, he found the lass who'd been haunting his thoughts all night standing not five feet away from him. She still wore the same jeans and hiking boots and hoodie, and her hands were shoved in the pockets.

"What are ye doing here, lass?"

Her chin lifted, nostrils flaring as she sniffed. "Actually, you smell like more than one."

Duncan didn't respond. What was there to say? She was right.

"Did you have fun?"

Something in her tone affected him deeply. "No, I did no'," he told her honestly.

"You smell like you had fun." Her head tilted to the side and her brow furrowed. "Although, I guess I would be more concerned if you only smelled like one human in particular. By walking out of the club drenched in so many odious perfumes, it tells me there wasn't a singular woman who kept your attention, but numerous women. And that tells me you were just blowing off steam, and not looking for my replacement."

Turning his back to her, he stuck his key in the door and unlocked it. "Ye dinna need tae be concerned at all. Ye are no' my keeper."

"I don't know what I did wrong."

Duncan looked heavenward, hoping the gods would take pity on him and send down a sudden storm. Perhaps with some dangerous lightning bolts.

But it appeared they'd turned their backs on him this night. He was on his own.

However, he didn't have to stay there.

Opening his door, he put one leg inside. Then he paused. "What are ye doin' here, Ryanne?"

"I just told you. I don't know what I did wrong, or why you're suddenly so cold toward me, but I'd like to talk it out. I'd like things to go back to how they were earlier today."

Earlier today he'd been balls deep in her sweet heat. Had that all been part of her plan? A way to keep him distracted while she extracted information out of him? She'd used him. Used his body for her pleasure and his mind for her amusement. "Shouldn't ye be worried aboot yer father, the prince?"

"Yes." There was no hesitation in her answer. "But here I am." As though that explained everything.

"Find another wolf tae fook with, princess. As I told ye, I appreciate what ye did for me, and so did th' ladies inside."

It was cruel. That last thing.

A stricken expression twisted her bonnie features and colors flashed from her eyes, but Duncan was not to be swayed by her tricks. "But I dinna need ye anymore. And ye have Cedric now tae fill ye in on our pack's business. Ye dinna need me anymore, either, so ye can stop pretending I mean anything good tae ye."

She stepped toward him. "I'm not pretending Duncan."

He growled at her approach and she stopped. "Good luck, princess," he told her as a way of goodbye.

"Stop calling me that."

"Why? Is that no' what ye are?"

When she didn't answer, he climbed the rest of the way in the Jeep and closed the door.

Ryanne stayed where she was.

Duncan ignored her and stuck the key in the ignition. He just wanted to go home and sleep off all the whiskey and disappointment weighing down his bones. He was tired, both physically and emotionally, and he needed time away from the sight and smell of her. He would not be used by her. Not anymore.

The burner phone in his glovebox rang just as he gripped the gear shift. Leaving the Jeep in park, he pulled it out. It was Cedric. Icy cold fingers spread through his gut. The only reason he'd be calling on this phone was when something really bad had happened and he didn't want the call seen or traced.

Duncan threw the Jeep into drive as he answered. "Aye, Cedric, I'm on my way...what?" He stomped on the break before he managed to go anywhere and glanced out of the corner of his eye. Ryanne still stood where he had left her. Not that he needed to look to confirm it. He could feel her eyes on him. Feel the chaos of her emotions, as muddled as his own. "Aye, I do ken where she is. She's right here."

His heart stopped as he listed to his alpha, only to start back up again twice as fast. His voice was little more than a growl when he answered, "Aye. I've got her. He will no' find her. Aye, I'll check in when we get somewhere. Aye. I will." Ending the call, he laid the phone on the dash and smashed his fist down on it. Scooping it into his hand, he dropped it in the cup holder then rolled down his window. "Get in," he told Ryanne.

She didn't hesitate. Jogging around the front of the vehicle to the passenger side, she jumped in and buckled her seatbelt. "What's happened?" she asked as he pulled out of the parking lot.

"Yer father," was the only answer he gave her. And, apparently, that was the only response she needed, for she let out a breath and leaned back in the seat. Turning her head, she stared out the window.

Duncan headed south. The pack had a safe house on the northern tip of Bainbridge Island, but it was too late to take the ferry. He would go south through Tacoma and take the bridge across, then north to Poulsbo and back south to the tip of the island. It was the long way, but it would have to do. He needed to get her away from the pack.

They drove in silence until they got across the bridge. Once on the other side, Duncan pulled off the highway.

Ryanne sat up, looking out the windows. "Why are we stopping?"

"I need tae get gas and a few supplies." Duncan heard the way he clipped off his words, but he couldn't help it. He was angry. He just didn't know if it was at her, or at himself for being taken for such a fool.

"Oh." Settling back in her seat, she went back to staring out the window.

His conscience pricked at him, but there was no time to get into some heartfelt discussion. Pulling into a grocery store, he stopped at the pumps and filled up the Jeep, then pulled up into the parking lot. "Stay in the vehicle," he ordered. Reaching across her lap, he pulled another burner phone out of the glovebox, ignoring the heat that speared through him when he accidentally brushed her thigh. "If anything happens, dial the number one on the speed dial. Ye ken how tae do that?"

She took the phone, pressed the home button, checked out the screen. She nodded.

"Good. Th' keys are in th' ignition. If anything happens, anyone gets too close, ye leave. Do ye hear me? Ye leave, and ye call me on that phone."

"What about you?"

"I will find ye," he told her. Opening his door, he jumped out. "Keep th' doors locked," he told her, then he pushed the button to do just that and shut the door.

Walking into the store, he felt the weight of her gaze as she watched him.

Duncan steeled his spine, ignoring the howls of his wolf for leaving her alone and unprotected. He ground his teeth together.

She was not his to protect. Not now. Not ever.

CHAPTER 19

The silence was becoming oppressive by the time they pulled off the one lane road they'd been driving on for the last eight or so miles.

Ryanne had never been so happy to get out of a vehicle.

She looked around. It was still dark, but she could smell the fishy, salty air of the Puget Sound. And by the sound of water lapping against the shoreline, this was a waterfront property. Trees towered around the property on the remaining three sides, hiding them from anyone who might be passing by.

Surveying the little, brown, one-story house, she was surprised to spot cameras on each corner of the roof. And as she watched, they moved slowly in an arc, scanning the area.

Duncan walked past her, his arms full of paper bags. Ryanne followed him across the long porch to the front door, where a panel with numbered buttons kept anyone from getting in. She tried to watch as he punched in a code, but he stepped to the side to block her view before opening the door and walking inside. Ever the gentleman, even when he was upset with her, he held the door open with his foot, waiting for her to pass him before he let it swing shut.

He nodded to her right, and she headed that way.

Setting the bags on the small, round table just off the rustic kitchen, he flicked on a light. Pausing on his way back out to the Jeep, he said, "There's a couple o' bedrooms down th' hall there." He pointed behind her. "Pick whichever one ye like. If ye'd like tae shower or anything, there's clean towels and such in th' hall closet. Spare clothes are in th' closet in the bedroom. Either one. They're no' yer size, but ye may be able tae find something ye can wear until we can get ye something."

After he left, she pulled her hoodie off and draped it over a chair, looking around. The kitchen was done in different shades of natural woods—the floor, the cabinets, the counters, even the table. Large, square windows lined the wall behind the table—a theme throughout the house she soon found out—and she would bet the views during the daylight hours were stunning. The appliances were stainless steel and probably on the higher end of the price range, if she were to take a guess.

Peeking in one of the bags, she found canned soups, peanut butter, jelly, and a thick loaf of some kind of grainy bread on top.

In the other bag there was some apples and oranges and pre-packaged salads. She started pulling them out and putting them in the fridge, noticing it was already stocked with just about every condiment one could want. She wondered whose house this was, and how often someone was here.

If this were her house, with the trees and the water and complete lack of neighbors—human or otherwise—she didn't think she would ever want to leave.

Duncan came back inside, saw her standing there with a couple of cans of soup in her hand and stopped short before he seemed to catch himself. Continuing forward, he placed the last two bags on the table. As he began to unpack the packages of meat from one and bags of frozen stuff from another, he said, "Dinna ye want tae ken why we're here? Or do ye trust me that much?"

The last was said in jest, she knew, but she answered him honestly all the same. "I do trust you."

He eyed her as he pulled what looked to be large steaks out of the last bag. "And what if yer wrong?"

"I'm not."

"How do ye ken?"

"I'm not," she insisted. "And I wish you would stop and just talk to me. You're upset. And I know why. But if you would just talk to me—"

The door to the refrigerator slammed shut, and Ryanne jumped in spite of her herself.

"Ye want tae ken why I'm upset?" he asked through clenched teeth. "Ye want me tae spell it out for ye?"

"Please," she told him. Pulling out a chair, she sat down at the table, crossed her legs, folded her hands on the table-top, and waited. Ryanne couldn't stand the tension between them anymore. She wasn't used to it, being that she'd spent most of her time alone ever since her father had tried to kill her. She didn't know how to process it.

And it hurt.

Duncan eyed her sitting there with narrowed eyes but didn't join her. Instead, he paced the small space of the kitchen, much like Cedric had earlier in his apartment. Only unlike Cedric, who had done it out of habit while he was thinking, Duncan seemed to be doing it to work out the aggression rolling under his skin. She knew this because she could feel it thickening the air. And by the way he rolled the tension from his shoulders and cracked his neck from side to side.

"Do you want me to start?" she asked.

He stopped pacing and stared at her. A muscle ticked in his jaw. "Ye used me."

"Duncan—"

With a quick shake of his head, he cut her off before she could try to explain. "No. Ye dinna get tae give me yer excuses. Ye used me for information about my pack and yer father's place within it."

"You're right," she told him. "I did."

"Aye, ye did. But I'm done being used. For information or…anything else."

Anything else? What did that mean?

His chest rose and fell on a deep inhale. "I'm going tae bed," he announced. And he did, indeed, sound tired. "I suggest ye do the same. Yer safe here. The house and grounds are monitored twenty-four hours. I've set th' alarm on th' house and there's an invisible fence around th' property. Dinna try tae sneak out or th' alarms will sound."

"What if I want to go outside and get some air?"

"Ye can go outside tomorrow," was his short response.

Ryanne watched him walk away, a heaviness in her chest she didn't know how to deal with. She wanted to fix things between them, but she didn't know how.

He was absolutely right. She had used him for information. In the beginning, at least. And her need to get to know him had been for purely selfish reasons. But she wasn't sorry she'd done so.

For a long time now, there was only one person Ryanne could depend on, and that was herself. The only one she could trust was herself. Not friends. And certainly not family. Her very life depended on it. And she wouldn't apologize for it.

She just wished he would understand why she'd done what she had and not take it so personally. It had nothing to do with him, and everything to do with her own survival.

The life she had as good as sacrificed when she started to care more about being with a shifter then watching her own back.

A huge sigh escaped her. Perhaps he was right to cut off whatever this was between them now, before it completely ruined everything.

Yes, she decided as she rummaged around for a teabag, Duncan was right. And she needed to stop…whatever this was she was feeling for him and concentrate on the reason she was here. Perhaps Cedric could send out another of his pack to stay with her, though. Because she didn't know how strong her resolve would be after days or weeks in such close proximity with Duncan.

Finally, she found a box of tea bags and she smiled. She hadn't had a hot cup of tea in months. A tea pot sat on the stovetop, and she filled it with water and turned on a burner to heat it. Soon, she was turning off the light and walking down the hall, a steaming cup of tea in her hand.

She listened for something to tell her which room Duncan had taken, and finally heard him moving around in the room to her left. Turning on her heel, she entered the one across the hall. In the darkness, she saw the outline of a large bed with a little table next to it. The table contained a lamp. The room was otherwise empty.

As she'd taken a shower earlier at Duncan's, she didn't bother to do so now. Besides, it appeared the only bathroom was at the end of the hall between the two rooms, and she didn't want to give him any reason to yell at her more. Not until she had time to think through everything he'd said in the kitchen. Instead, she stripped down to her underwear and her thermal shirt and climbed into bed without bothering to turn on the light.

Sipping her tea, she watched the moon descend into the trees outside her window.

She wished she could open it so she could smell the ocean air and feel the breeze.

· · ·

Something woke Ryanne from a sound sleep. Startled, she sat up, not remembering at first where she was. Rubbing her eyes, she looked around the room.

Brown comforter. Brown sheets. Single lamp on a bedside table. Large, square window on the wall to her left. But no moon this time as the clouds had rolled in again.

The little, brown house with her shifter sleeping across the hall instead of in her bed.

Sitting very still, she listened. Rain pattered on the roof and a tree branch rubbed against the house somewhere. Nothing that would've woken her. And thunder was not common in this area. Just the steady rain that never failed to lull her to sleep.

She must have been dreaming.

Ryanne scooted back down into the bed. Sat up again. Took a sip of her now-cold tea. Then snuggled back under the thick blankets. It was no wonder she'd slept so hard. The thing was like a giant cloud, cradling her body perfectly.

Thirty seconds later, she threw off the blankets and padded in her bare feet to the bathroom. She was washing her hands and had just shut the water off when she heard it again. A moan, eerie and drawn out, filled with such agony it raised the hair on the back of her neck.

Quietly, she opened the door and stepped into the hall. Was someone in the house?

The sound came again, only this time with a muffled shout accompanying it.

It was coming from Duncan's room.

Reacting on instinct alone, she rushed to his door and

threw it open. But there were no invaders. No one had broken in. She only saw Duncan in a bed much like hers, the blankets twisted around his legs as he thrashed beneath them.

Ryanne walked quickly to the bed, not knowing what to do. Should she wake him? She didn't want to scare him.

He mumbled something she couldn't understand, his face twisting into a mask of pain that pulled at things inside of her. Things she'd never known were there. Things that made her hurt as he was obviously hurting, if only in his memories.

That made up her mind. She would not leave him locked in the prison of his mind to fight his demons alone. For she had a good idea exactly who they were, and she couldn't help but feel somewhat responsible. Ryanne knew what it was like to be a prisoner of her people, and she hated knowing he was going through that. Even if it wasn't real this time.

"Duncan." She touched his bare arm, blinking hard against the wetness in her eyes. "Duncan, wake up. It's only a dream."

Turning on the bedside light, she saw his eyes moving back and forth beneath his eyelids. His lips moved, murmuring things she couldn't hear or understand. Ryanne sat on the edge of the bed and took both of his shoulders in her hands.

The thick muscles tensed beneath her touch.

"Duncan! Wake up!" she said a little louder. "Wake up. It's only a dream." She gave him a little shake. "Duncan!"

On a rasping inhale, his eyes shot open and stared at the ceiling for a brief second before zeroing in on her face.

She gave him a small smile. "It's okay. You were having a dream."

He was very still. Only his eyes moved as they travelled over her face.

A shadow passed within them, and it wasn't Duncan looking out at her. Ryanne sat up, putting a little distance between herself and the beast staring out at her.

It didn't look happy with her.

She lowered her eyes—not quite knowing why except that something told her to do it—and saw the colorful rainbow of her emotions reflecting off the dark comforter.

There was a menacing snarl, and suddenly hands were around her upper arms and she was flipped around and thrown onto her back.

Duncan loomed over her, his teeth bared, showing white in the darkness. "Ye think ye can make me less a male with yer sick games," he gritted out. "But ye will no' fookin' win. Do ye hear me? No' while I'm alive."

"I'm not trying to hurt you, Duncan. You were dreaming." Ryanne's heart raced, making her lightheaded. For the first time since she'd known him, she was honestly worried he would hurt her. It was not her shifter staring down at her, but a male fighting to survive, lost in the world of his nightmares. "It's me. Ryanne. I know you're angry with me, but I would never try to hurt you. You're safe with me. It's okay." She just kept talking, hoping she'd get through to the cognizant part of him.

He didn't appear to hear her.

Or maybe he did and, lost in his memories, saw her only as the enemy. An enemy that needed to be taken out.

Ryanne felt the vibrations of her dark magic pulsing inside of her. She didn't want to use it against him, but she would if it came down to her own survival. "Duncan…"

"No!" he growled. "No."

His mouth crashed onto hers, forcing her submission until she opened for him and let him in. Until she let him ravish her mouth with lips and tongue and teeth.

Ryanne moaned. She couldn't help it. The wildness inside of him spoke to her own dark nature, not in whispered sweet nothings meant to coax her passion, but with a dominate command she could not refuse and didn't want to.

He broke off the kiss with a nip of his teeth that drew blood. "Ye have no' broken me, soul sucker. And I will prove it tae ye." Straddling her hips, he sat up and gripped the neckline of her thermal shirt. With a quick yank, he tore it in two, letting it fall to either side and exposing her bare breasts to his angry gaze.

Tilting his head to the side, he stared down at her for long moments. Then, with both hands, he trailed his fingers down over her collarbone and around the curves of each breast before taking them in his hands and squeezing. Hard.

He took the hard buds of her nipples between his thumb and forefinger, tightening the clamps they made until pleasure and pain shot straight to her womb.

The air stuck in her lungs as she tried to draw a breath,

her nails digging into his knees. By all the gods, she'd never been stared at so, like he wanted to rip her limb from limb and fuck her while he was doing it. If she didn't keep her head about her, that very well may happen.

She had no more time to think as Duncan pushed away from her to stand and remove his boxer briefs. His manhood sprung free from a nest of dark curls, thick and long and hard.

Her thighs clenched and she felt a rush of moisture, her body preparing to accept him.

However, he would have none of that. Prying her legs apart, he ripped her underwear off, not caring when there was the distinctive sound of something tearing.

He stood over her, his chest rising and falling with fast, deep breaths and his hand wrapped around his length. As she watched, he slid his hand down and up, tightening his grip at the wide head. With a grin that was evil and satisfying, he grabbed her ankles. A quick twist and she was on her stomach.

Duncan grabbed her hips, pulling her up onto her knees so her ass was in the air. The remainder of her shirt was torn from her back. His hands were on her hips and she felt him probing at her entrance.

With a low growl, he pushed inside of her.

Ryanne gasped. She wasn't quite ready, and it hurt. But if he heard her, he didn't seem to care as he began to move, pulling nearly all the way out slowly only to thrust inside of her again hard. She gripped the sheets, hanging on for dear life. In no time at all the discomfort went away as her body stretched to accept him.

His hands squeezed her hips so hard she knew she was going to have the indentions of his fingers there for hours afterward. But she didn't care. He may be working out his demons, but Ryanne was more than happy to help him do it as the little muscles in her lower stomach tightened. Reaching between her torso and the bed, she found she was wet with need. With her own hand, she helped her body find the pleasure it was seeking, crying out and pushing her hips back to meet him when her orgasm hit her.

Her pleasure only seemed to anger him more. A spine-chilling snarl sounded in her ear, his breath leaving chills on the back of her neck as Duncan crushed her down to the bed with his weight, pounding into her from behind.

Wrapping his fist in her loose curls, he twisted her head around. "Open yer eyes soul sucker, and look at who is fuckin' ye now."

Ryanne did as he told her, wanting more than anything in the world to give him the satisfaction he was seeking. It was little enough. Something she could do to help him. And she was happy to sacrifice herself in this way that brought them both so much pleasure.

As he buried himself deep in her body with a yell of triumph and she felt his seed pumping into her, Ryanne felt tears fill her eyes and shut them tight. Not wanting him to see.

To her surprise, he didn't order her to open them again, but collapsed on top of her. Holding most of his weight on his elbows, his forehead fell to the bed beside hers. His chest heaved against her back and his hard breaths rasped in her ear.

She lay quietly with him still inside of her, enjoying the feel of their sweat-slickened bodies and wondering what she could say to fix what was wrong between them. Because Ryanne had no doubt he was still angry with her. However, she wanted more with this male than to be a vessel for his needs when he had demons to fight. She cared about him. And she believed, underneath all of this, he also felt something for her.

Eventually, he lifted his head and his hand loosened its grip in her hair, combing through the curls as he released her. "Ryanne."

She tried to read his tone, but it was impossible. Lifting her eyes to his face, she sought more information from his expression.

When her eyes met his, his widened in horror. She quickly dropped them again, hiding them behind her eyelids and wishing like hell she could control the damn colors that spooked him so much.

But she was too late. Cold air rushed over her naked body as he practically leapt off of her. She rolled over, noticing his eyes rake over her.

"Och, Ryanne. What th' fook are ye doing in here?"

He sounded angry. Disgusted. And a hole opened up in her chest as she tried to speak around the thickness in her throat. "You were having a nightmare."

"A nightmare."

She nodded, unable to say anymore and still afraid to look at him.

Long seconds went by. Then, without a word, he turned and left the room. A second later she heard the bathroom door slam and the water come on.

She looked around the room without actually seeing it. Was she so repulsive to him? Had she completely misread him?

As she thought it through, she bit her lower lip and felt the blood drain from her face. She'd been a fool. Her earlier thinking was completely wrong. He didn't smile at her with that easy grin like he did with other females. He didn't wink. He didn't tease. He didn't flirt.

He stared at her like she was about to grow horns and drag him down to the Christian's hell to spend eternity in what she now knew were his nightmares.

And he fucked her when she worked him up to it or when he wanted to use her to prove, thanks to her, that her people hadn't broken him. That he was still a male.

She horrified him.

Red hot anger filled the whole in her chest. Ryanne climbed out of his bed and used her discarded shirt to clean herself off. She wasn't going to sit here and wait for him to come out just so she could see the disgust in his eyes and see the tension in the way he held himself around her.

Marching back to her room, she rooted around in the closet until she found a black, heavy pullover shirt. Unfortunately, the only pants were jeans that were tight around her hips and ass and way too long. But after she folded them up into cuffs at the bottom, they weren't too bad. Moving fast now, she found her socks and boots and put them on, then went out to the kitchen and helped herself to the sandwich makings and fruit.

At the door, she paused. The alarms would go off when she left, and there was nothing she could do to stop it. She didn't know the code. And she knew without a doubt Duncan would be hot on her heels as soon as left. Not because he cared, but because those were the orders his alpha gave him.

Think, Ryanne. Think.

The water shut off in the bedroom. She was out of time.

With one last, longing look down the hallway, she unlocked the door, pulled it open, and ran out the door.

CHAPTER 20

Duncan stood under the warm spray of the shower, his hands braced on the tiles as the water flowed over his head and down his body.

Horror filled him. And shame. But mostly horror.

He couldn't believe what had just happened. What he had just done. When he'd gone to bed, he'd been angry, aye. But that was no excuse for how he'd reacted to finding her in his room, even if he had still been lost in the throes of the dream he'd been having.

How was he to face her after acting like such a beast?

Knowing he couldn't put if off forever and thinking he may as well rip off the band aid, he turned off the water and grabbed the nearest towel. Luckily there had already been a couple of them hanging in the bathroom, or he'd be drip drying right now.

An alarm began to beep throughout the house, pulling Duncan from his thoughts of self-disgust. Fear shot through him at such a rate that for a moment, he was completely frozen. "Fookin' hell!"

That was the interior alarm. They'd been found.

Wrapping the towel around his waist, he threw open the bathroom door and ran back to his room, heart pounding in his chest even as a cold calm coming over his thoughts. He would get her out and to safety. And then he would apologize for acting like he had and pray to all of the gods she could forgive him.

But when he got there, the door to his room was open and Ryanne was gone. "Ryanne!"

Duncan ran to the closet and threw on a pair of jeans, yelling over the alarm. "Ryanne! Lass, where are ye?" Barefoot and bare chested, he ran to her room, thinking she must be searching for something to cover herself.

It was empty.

"Ryanne!" Icy fingers crept through him, settling into a block of ice in his chest. Stopping in the middle of the hall, he forced himself to calm as he listened. But he heard nothing except the loud beeping of now both the interior *and* exterior alarms and a light drizzle of rain on the roof.

Wait.

The interior alarm had gone off first.

He began to search the house, hoping he was wrong.

But he wasn't wrong. She was gone. He'd frightened her off with his heartless brutality. Shame weighed heavy on his shoulders, but he shook it off. He would bellow his sorrows and beat himself up later. Right now, he needed to find her and make sure she was safe.

Punching in the code, he cut off the alarms and cracked open the front door. Carefully, he looked out, scanning the immediate area just in case he was wrong in his assumptions. When no one jumped him, he opened it wider and stepped out onto the porch. He caught the slightest whiff of primroses lingering in the air. Backing up, he smelled the wood of the doorframe right about at the level of her head. The scent was stronger there, like her riotous hair had brushed it on her way out. "Damn it!" His fist punched the wall, leaving a hole, and he slammed the door.

But what if she'd been taken? Someone could've come to the door and tricked her...

He immediately dismissed the idea. His Ryanne was a smart lass. She would never fall for something so obvious. And if that had been the way of it, the outside alarm would have sounded as soon as someone crossed over onto the property.

Back in his room, he found his boots and a dark, clean shirt. A light raincoat hung in the closet, but he left it there. It would help keep him dry, but the crinkling sounds of the material would only give him away. Besides, he didn't mind the rain. The only bad thing about it was that he needed to hurry before it completely washed away her trail.

Outside, he locked up the house but didn't reset the alarms in case she came back. A busted door could be replaced. The alarms would alert anyone within a few miles and would draw unwanted attention, especially with the sun coming up soon. Though the house was located at the very tip of the island, there were humans just south of them.

The safe house hid in plain sight, surrounded by enough woodland to hide them if needed, but close enough to the regular population to be overlooked by those who might mean them harm.

At his Jeep, Duncan pulled out a burner phone. He started dialing Cedric, stopped, backed out of the call, and put the phone in his front pocket. His lass had a good head start. Even on foot, she could run at a speed that rivaled only the vampires, but there was no way in hell he wasn't going to find her.

Leaving his Jeep where it is, he searched for her trail. The rain was letting up, but it was still falling in a nice drizzle typical of this part of the country. Rain be damned, he found her footprints near the water and followed them for a good mile or so. When he had a good idea of where he was going, he ran back to the house and got in his Jeep.

Ryanne was following the water's edge. She probably thought it would help cover her scent, and it did. But not enough to hide her from him. And she was obviously in too much of a hurry to think about the trail she was leaving in the soft ground.

Knowing the direction she went, he now had a good idea where he would find her. She could outrun him on foot. But she wouldn't outrun Vina.

Fifteen minutes later, as the sunrise was sparkling on the water, he pulled up to the ferry that would take him back over to Seattle. Leaving his vehicle in the line waiting to board, he walked up to where those without a car were waiting, looking for her dark curls.

But Ryanne wasn't there.

Fighting down the panic, he backtracked the way she would've came. There was no sign that she had made it this far.

He'd been positive this was where she had headed. Was the lass hiding on the island somewhere? But that didn't make sense. If she'd wanted to escape him, she knew he would look for her, and she also knew he would sniff her out if she was anywhere nearby.

Rushing back to his Jeep, he pulled out of line, drove over the curb and went back the way he'd came, using the roads that hugged the coastline as best as he could this time. Every few minutes, he'd pull over and walk to the water, searching for some sign of her.

His gut was beginning to ache, tied up in ropes as it was. What if he'd been wrong? What if she hadn't run but been taken right out from under his roof while he'd been hiding in the bathroom like a coward?

No. He couldn't think like that. He would find her. And she would only be hiding as he'd thought. Perhaps she only thought to scare him. To teach him a lesson.

A few miles up the road, he finally thought he caught her scent on the bark of a tree in a wooded area mostly hidden from the houses. He walked south along the coastline a little ways and lost it. Turning back north he picked it up again and followed it back toward the road. He lost it again before he was free of the trees.

It was like she'd disappeared into thin air.

That icy feeling came back to his chest. There was only

creature he knew who came and went through time and space on nothing more than a whim.

The Faerie prince.

Duncan's vision blurred as the world spun around him. Bracing his hands on his knees, he forced air into his lungs. When he could breathe enough to speak, he pulled out his phone and dialed Cedric, still bent over. "He's got her," he told him as soon as his alpha answered. "He's got my lass."

Rising to his full height, one hand pulled at his hair as his teeth ground together. "It's my fault, Cedric. It's my fookin' fault." His voice broke on the last sentence.

A few seconds later, he snapped the phone in his hand and tossed it on the ground. A howl of pain and rage boiled up within him, and he covered his face with his hands, releasing it all into his palms. His wolf prowled beneath his skin, its teeth bared, aching to rip into the prince for taking its mate.

Slowly, Duncan straightened and ran his hands through his wet hair. He hadn't felt the rain that was now coming down heavier, cold and wet on his head. He didn't hear the water lapping against the shore. Nor the distant sounds of the humans as they left their houses and headed off to start their days.

Mine. The lass is mine.

His wolf growled in agreement as Duncan's jaw clenched. Och, aye. Why had he not seen it before?

Because he'd been too caught up in what happened in the past and blaming her for it. For something she hadn't participated in or even known about.

He moved his head from side to side, stretching the muscle and easing the tension. With purpose now, he strode back to his Jeep.

Ryanne needed him. And he would not let her down again.

AN HOUR AND A HALF LATER, he pulled into the parking lot of his apartment complex.

Brock waited for him just inside the entrance.

"Where is Cedric?" Duncan asked him.

"He's out with the others."

His surprise was so great, Duncan came to an abrupt halt in the middle of the hall to stare at the young wolf. "He's out looking for Ryanne?"

"Yup. And so are the girls. They figure they found Bronaugh while we ran around the mountains like a bunch of idiots, so maybe they could find the prince's daughter, too."

He gave Brock a level stare. "Cedric told ye aboot her."

"Yeah, he filled us all in right after you called."

Duncan nodded. "She's mine, ye ken."

Brock smiled. "Of course, she is. Otherwise why would we be going through all of this trouble?"

With a nod, Duncan proceeded down the hall.

"Where are you going?" Brock asked as they neared the stairs.

"To get a few things and find my lass," Duncan told him as he neared the door. "Did Cedric tell ye where he went?"

"No, but I got the feeling he wanted you to hang tight here. I was told to stay with you. He said he would get word to us as soon as he could."

"Ye ken Cedric is out o' his damn mind if he thinks I'm going tae sit here while my lass is out there all alone somewhere? Possibly hurt? Or worse?" This last was nothing but a rasp torn from his throat.

"Yup, I know that."

"So, ye ken I'm going after her and ye can no' stop me?"

Brock pulled a hair band out of his pocket and started pulling back his long, wavy hair. "I know that, too."

"Are ye coming, then?"

"Oh, yeah. I've already got supplies ready to load up in Vina. Including some spare clothes. I figured we'd start out driving and go wolf when we need to."

"Where is everything?"

"My apartment, just inside the door."

Duncan slapped him on the shoulder. "Yer a good one, Brock."

Grabbing the door, Brock held it open and indicated for him to go first. "After you, Duncan."

True to his word, it seemed Brock had, indeed, thought of everything. Not only had he packed enough food and water for days, he had three changes of clothes for each of them, and even a couple of wicked looking blades.

Duncan picked one up, admiring the way it balanced in his hand. "What do ye plan on doing with these? Ye can no' kill a Faerie as powerful as the prince with a knife."

"I know, but I feel better having them along."

An icy shiver ran down his spine, and Duncan put it back. "We need tae hurry."

Brock didn't question him, just jogged over to the passenger side and got in. "Do you know where we're going?" he asked when Duncan climbed in beside him.

Another shiver crawled along the back of his neck, like someone was watching him. But a quick look in the rearview mirror proved no one was behind him. Only a past version of himself, begging him not to go.

"Aye," he told Brock. "I believe I do."

Throwing Vina into drive, he spun around and tore out of the apartments.

When he hit the main road, he took a deep breath, braced himself, and headed east.

CHAPTER 21

R yanne stared across the wide cavern at the man who had helped bring her into being. She wasn't really surprised that, somehow, he'd know exactly where she was, and he'd swooped in and taken her away the first chance he'd gotten.

Tired of waiting for him to say something, she let her attention wander. Actually, this secret hideaway of his was more of a cave than a cavern. It wasn't completely under-ground. It was hidden behind the waterfall she could hear in the distance. The roar of the water filled the silence and weighed down the air with moisture, causing moss to cover the stone. But overall, it was a rather pleasant sound.

Still, this father/daughter bonding experience would be more to her liking if she weren't being held there against her will. One could argue that as there were no physical bindings holding her in place, that was not the case. Yet, the four turned werewolves surrounding her were a great deterrent in case she had any thoughts of trying to make a run for it. Two of them she recognized as the survivors from the night Duncan was attacked. The others were new to her, but she assumed they were also from Thomas's pack. New recruits, perhaps.

With nothing else to distract her, she turned her attention back to her father.

The prince, with his long, white hair and unlined face, looked exactly the same as he had the last time she'd seen him. This was no surprise to Ryanne. He had been ancient before she'd been born and if he followed a Faerie's natural life span, it was to be expected he would live many more years.

But not if she had anything to say about it.

Duana, the reigning princess of the *an olc*, stood to his right. She was staring at Ryanne like she'd just grown another head.

"What's wrong, sister?" Ryanne asked her. "Didn't our father tell you I was still alive?"

She said nothing for a long time. Without taking her eyes from Ryanne, she told her, "No. No, he did not. But unless you've changed your opinion of your own people, your being here is an obstruction in our plans we really don't need right now."

"Now you're starting to sound like our father."

"Well, I am his daughter."

As if she wasn't. "Sorry to upset things by being, you know, alive and all that."

Duana narrowed her eyes at her and made a small noise

in the back of her throat that said she took Ryanne's apology exactly how she'd meant it. Which was not at all.

Prince Nada finally decided to join the conversation, his tone calm, almost conversational. "How much have you told the wolf?"

"About what, exactly?"

"Don't be coy," he told her. "You know exactly what I am referring to."

Ryanne very nearly blurted out that Duncan—and now Cedric—knew very nearly everything. But that probably wouldn't be the best move. However, she also couldn't lie. The prince had an uncanny ability of pulling out the truth, especially where deep emotions were concerned.

And her emotions for Duncan ran very deep, indeed.

"I told him I was your daughter. And I told him you thought I was dead, that I'd died during the last war." All true. "And I told him I was here to stop you from releasing the ones who need to stay in their own world." She let her eyes flicker over to her sister for a split second before they returned to her father. Hopefully, it would give him the impression that last statement was aimed at Duana, and not of him, as Duana's part in this game was well known by the wolves.

"Has he told his pack?"

"I don't know."

"Has he seen your eyes, child?"

That question stopped her for a brief second. Almost violently, she pushed the memories of Duncan screaming in the mud, out of her head. Kittens. Think of kittens. Cute, sweet, tiny kittens with blue eyes. Little hellions with sharp claws and teeth. "Not that I know of."

The prince was silent.

Ryanne never took him from her line of sight, never broke the connection, and thought about kittens.

She felt no which way about the little furballs. Could take them or leave them.

Eventually, he released a sigh of relief. "Good. That's good. I'm glad you still have a smidgeon of sense." He smiled at Duana. "She must get that from me."

Rolling her eyes, Ryanne spotted a large rock and took a step to her left to sit on it.

Deep growls and snapping teeth forced her to a stop. "I just want to sit down," she snapped back.

"Let her," the prince told them, and the wolves took a step back in synchronicity. Almost like they were on strings, and the prince was their master.

This did not surprise Ryanne in the least. He'd had Thomas and his pack on leashes for years. First, leading up to the war. And now leading up to the release of the Faeries he, himself, had banished. Glaring at the gray wolf closest to her, she walked over and sat down with a grateful sigh.

"Tell me exactly all that has transpired between you and Duncan," her father ordered.

"I really don't see how that's any of your concern."

He tilted his head, and a dangerous smile played around his mouth. "It is my concern if you've put myself or our people in any danger. So, you see, I must insist on prying, daughter, for the good of all involved." He waved a hand in the air like he was waving away a bad smell. "You don't need to tell me all of the gory details. You've always had a soft heart for those who are troubled."

"Troubled?" she repeated. Ryanne very nearly laughed out loud. "Is that what you call it when you probe so deep into a male's psyche, when you produce so much fear at the mere thought of being sexually aroused, that he completely believes he is only half the male he once was? And why? Just to prove that you can?"

"Sort of," the prince said pleasantly. "It was an experiment, you see. The wolves have higher than normal levels of testosterone. We wanted to see if unmanning one would change his loyalty to his pack or lesson his need to shift. Lesson his urge to fight. To protect. All of those caveman-like qualities they're known for."

"Why mess with his head? Why not just castrate him?" she asked. And she thought she did a pretty good job of keeping her tone casual. The very thought horrified her, but she had to ask.

"Oh, no, dear. We wouldn't want to actually hurt one of our allies like that. As it was, Cedric found him before we could temper the trauma. He wouldn't have been nearly as affected as he was—mentally, I mean—if we had been allowed to finish what we'd started."

"You can remove the memories, but you weren't going to fix what you did."

He appeared to really think about that for the first time. "Perhaps, eventually. After we monitored his behavior for a few years."

She studied her nails. They were dirty again. As much time as she spent in the wilderness, Ryanne was a stickler for clean nails. "Well, father, I'm not sorry to say I completely messed up your experiment. The results will now be skewed, to say the least."

He sighed heavily and tapped the tip of his cane on the rock beneath his feet. "You always were selfish that way. Trying to save the world, one pathetic individual at a time, instead of worrying about what you should have been concerned with."

"Which is?"

"Our people, Ryanne," Duana nearly shouted. "Our people! Not the *na maithe* tribe, not the shifters, not the vampires or witches or even the humans."

The prince put his hand on her sister's arm. "Duana please. There's no need for such theatrics. As long as Ryanne hasn't told anyone what she actually is, nothing has changed."

Duana looked at him like he'd lost his mind. "Has she met the other Faeries who are living in that building, sleeping with those dogs? Because if she has, then they not only know who she is, but what she is. And by extension, what you are."

With an obliging expression, the prince turned back to Ryanne. "Have you met any of the other Faeries who are mated to some of the wolves in Cedric's pack, dear?"

"No," she told him.

"And we're supposed to believe you fucked that wolf and

he didn't see the colors in your eyes?" her sister asked. "Was he that bad?"

Anger rose up in Ryanne, so swift and sudden the rush made her lightheaded.

"Och, dinna knock it until ye try it, lass."

All heads turned as Duncan strolled into the cave, wearing only a pair of faded jeans.

Seeing him there, in this place, and knowing what it had to cost him to be there…panic rose within her.

He had returned to his nightmare for her.

Ryanne swiftly lowered her gaze to her lap, knowing her emotions would show in her eyes. She kept them there until she was certain she had them under control. If her father saw her reaction to Duncan, he would manipulate her emotions against both of them.

Pulling a blanket of impassiveness around her, she raised her eyes.

Duncan didn't look her way. Instead, his glowing green eyes skated right over the prince and landed on Duana.

Ryanne fought back a grin. The insult was not missed by his royal ego-ness.

Duncan lowered his chin in greeting. "Princess."

She didn't return the greeting.

His eyes swiftly took her in, from the top of her head to her toes. "Ryanne, are ye all right, lass?"

He seemed okay. Was he okay? Leaning back on her rock, she stretched her legs out in front of her and crossed them at the ankles, mimicking his aura of calm. "I am."

One side of his mouth lifted in a smile, then he raised a

brow at the four wolves guarding her. "Who are yer friends?" He squinted at one of them and wagged his finger in his direction. "Wait, dinna I ken this one?"

"Yes," she answered. "I believe you kicked his ass that night they interrupted our date." She kept her tone playful. There was no need at all for everyone to know it was anything but that—a fun date.

"I believe yer right, Ryanne." Then, and only then, did he acknowledge the prince. "Prince Nada."

Her father had watched this entire exchange with an unhidden expression of delight. "Duncan!" he greeted him. "We were just talking about you."

"Aye, I ken that. Ye were blethering on so much aboot me, ye did no' hear me come in." He casually took another few steps closer to Ryanne. "But I heard every word."

That was the wrong thing to say.

Ryanne tried to catch his attention to warn him without seeming obvious about it, but he was watching her father. As he should be. The prince was not to be trusted. Ever.

"I'll be taking Ryanne out o' here, now," Duncan informed him. "I ken what ye have planned for her— although I have tae admit I did no' *truly* believe ye when ye first told me—and it's no' going tae happen, yer highness."

Stop talking.

Terrified her father would hurt him, Ryanne stood up, ignoring the warning growls of the wolves surrounding her. Dusting off her hands loudly by slapping them against her thighs, she ignored them. "Guess I'll be seeing you later."

She smiled at her father and sister. "Don't call me. I'll call you."

Her ploy worked. The prince's attention was now solely on her. The amusement fell from his face. "You can't leave yet, Ryanne. The fun is only getting started."

A low growl reverberated through the cave. Duncan stood, alone and fearless, against her father and sister. "Ye will no' harm a single curl on her wee head, prince."

The prince took a step forward, opening his mouth to challenge Duncan's statement.

Duana touched his arm, stopping him, and whispered something in his ear.

Ryanne risked a glance at Duncan. He was staring at her…and something in his eyes….

He was frightened.

But then he visibly swallowed. Running his eyes up and down her body, he clenched his jaw until she saw the muscles jump and turned his attention back to her father and sister.

She knew what it had taken him to come after her on his own, especially now that he knew it was her father who was responsible for what happened to him the first time.

Ryanne wanted to go over to him and rush him out of there. He shouldn't have come. She could handle her father. After all, he was still her father. There had to be some type of sentiment for her somewhere beneath it all.

The tap-tap-tap of a cane heading in her direction alerted her, and she quickly schooled her features into a bored expression before turning to face the prince.

When he reached her, he looked at her for a moment much like Duncan just had before he began to speak, never taking his eyes from her face. "How about a trade, Duncan? Or an exchange, if you will."

After a moment, Duncan's voice broke the silence. "I'm listening."

Ryanne had a very sick idea of where this was going. She shook her head. "No," she told her father. "Do not do this."

"It's only fair, daughter. As it was you who broke my experiment."

"You said it was Cedric. That he came here and freed Duncan before you could finish your head games."

"I only said he changed the variables, not that he'd ruined it. No. It was you who did that. By showing the wolf he was still very much a male before I could finish collecting my data."

He was making up this game as he went. She knew that. And as there were no rules, Ryanne also knew she had no way of winning.

Duncan hadn't moved from where he'd been standing just inside the cave. But when he spoke, only someone who knew him well would catch the spike of fear in his voice. But there were also steel chords of determination. He meant to save her, and nothing she said or did would stop him. "Tell me your terms, Prince Nada."

With an ugly smile, the prince named his terms, calling them out loud and clear. "You for my daughter. I will allow her to leave with these wolves, if you stay here in her place."

"No!" Ryanne felt the flash of heat in her eyes and knew they were spinning with colors.

Her father smiled.

The game was over.

She looked over at Duncan. "Don't do it, Duncan. He'll kill you for what you know."

Duncan stared into her eyes, his face unreadable. "Deal," he told the prince. "Let her go."

Her father widened his eyes to comical proportions. "Well, that was much easier than I thought it would be. What in the world did you do to this poor lad? Do you have something magical between your legs?"

"Hey!" Duncan shouted as he stepped forward.

Ryanne held out her hand to stop him. "That's disgusting," she told the prince. "You're my father."

"Yes, I am. And yet you came here to take my life."

"I came here to stop you with whatever means necessary."

"Because you are my daughter, you know nothing will stop me. Nothing except my death."

It was true. Ryanne lifted her chin. She would not let him make her feel some sort of misplaced guilt. "Yes. I am your daughter. So, you should've made sure the job was done right the first time, you bastard." Cold hatred flowed through her.

They stared at each other for long seconds. Ryanne's fingertips tingled with power.

"Don't try it," her father said. "Or I will kill him now while you watch." To the wolves who had suddenly stepped closer, he said, "Take my daughter out of here. You know what to do."

Her eyes flew to Duncan as she was herded past him.

"No!" he shouted. He bared his teeth at the prince. "This was no' our deal!"

"Oh, yes. Yes, it was. I offered you a trade, and you accepted. I never specified what Thomas's wolves were to do with her."

The last thing Ryanne heard was Duncan's roar of anger and grief as she was hustled out of the cave to the waterfall. The largest wolf shoved her with his body to the left and she saw a small foot path. Not having a choice, she followed it, blinking away the tears in her eyes so she didn't slip and tumble out through the curtain of water. She had no idea how far her fall would be, and unlike her father, neither she nor her sister could travel through space without the use of their feet.

Think. Think.

Her magic sputtered from her fingers. But there was no way she could take out all four of her guards before she was taken down herself.

She tried to turn around. Tried to run around them to go back and save Duncan. But each time, she was stopped with their large bodies and nips of their teeth. The last two had drawn blood, and the scent only seemed to excite them more.

Reasoning with them would do no good, so she didn't waste the energy. Her father had them well trained.

Alright, then. She would fight. She would wait until they

got to wherever they were going where there was no danger of her falling over a waterfall, and she would fight.

And she would win.

She had to. The only other outcome was not acceptable.

The sun was high in the sky when one of her escorts nipped her on the thigh, making her jump to the side where another one nipped her arm. She'd been trying to reach out to Duncan, to feel him so she would know he was still alive, so it took her a second to realize they wanted her to stop. And another few to comprehend what was happening.

By this time, Ryanne was bleeding from multiple wounds. As soon as one healed, another was created until most of her body stung with every shift of her clothing. She'd pulled inward, concentrating on her connection with Duncan and not the physical pain she was in. Yet, no matter how hard she tried, she couldn't feel him.

He was cut off from her.

Ryanne refused to acknowledge what this most likely meant. If her father was in his head, perhaps he'd set up some type of barrier between them so she would believe the worst and it would distract her. After all, that would make her easier to kill, wouldn't it?

With effort, she pulled herself back to the here and now, wincing with the pain she was only now feeling. Thomas's wolves were restless, waiting for the nod to attack from their leader.

Four wolves against one injured Faerie. The odds were not in her favor. But that was exactly what she was counting on.

Even though she thought she was prepared, the attack came from nowhere. One second, the wolves were shifting their weight back and forth while the largest one nipped at their haunches and made little sounds, egging them on.

And then they were on her.

Blue light flew from her fingers, and she managed to knock away the one in front and to the side before she was slammed into from behind and long, sharp teeth sank into the meat between her shoulder and neck. The only reason she wasn't immediately beheaded because she had twisted her body around as soon as she felt him hit her.

Ryanne refused to scream. She absolutely refused to give them that. It would only make it worse for her. And she needed to keep her wits if there was any chance at all of surviving.

So, she laid still while the wolf on her back chewed on her shoulder. Through her hair, which she'd never put up before she ran, she watched the others pace around her head, waiting for their turn.

A growl sounded somewhere to her right, and chaos erupted around her. What was going on? Were they fighting amongst themselves?

The wolf on her back gave her a shake, and she gritted her teeth, pushing aside the pain. He released her and she immediately rolled to her back, feeling a stick dig into her side as she reached out and grabbed each side of the wolf's head. Blue fire shot into his skull. He barked at her through bloody teeth, sharp cries that eventually got fewer and farther between until his eyes closed and his heavy weight listed to the side.

Ryanne let his body drop beside her, then sprang to her feet, blue light buzzing around her fingertips.

The sight that met her eyes was not what she'd expected.

Two new wolves had joined the fray and were making short work of the three smaller wolves. As she watched, a black wolf—the largest of them all—turned his eerie white-blue eyes on her. He stared at her for a brief second, then tossed his big head and dove back into the fight.

It was the alpha. Cedric.

She had no idea who the other wolf was, but she wasn't going to wait around to find out. Duncan needed her.

Running full speed, she made it back to him in record time, only slowing after she'd cleared the waterfall. Stepping lightly, she kept her back against the wall, listening for any sounds as she approached the cave.

But there was nothing. Panic overtook her and she slammed her hand over her mouth to keep from giving away her presence.

Logic told her she was seeing an empty cave. Her heart told her he was still near.

Had the prince moved him? Taken him somewhere else? Was he...?

No, she wouldn't even think it.

Carefully, she stepped into the light. Her entire body trembling with fear and fatigue, she scanned the room, hoping for a clue. A scuff mark on the rock. Something.

What she found was far more.

Duncan kneeled alone in the middle of the room, arms straight out, held in midair by invisible threads. His head was up and his green eyes were wide and dark with terror, his mouth twisted, frozen in a silent scream. Sweat covered his face and neck and dampened the hair on his chest.

Quickly, she looked around. But her father and sister were nowhere to be seen. Still, she didn't move, but waited, searching through the connection they shared by blood.

They weren't there. Perhaps they knew Cedric had shown up and ran.

Ryanne ran across the cave to him, fully expecting her father to appear any moment and snatch her away from him. When she finally made it to Duncan—what felt like years later but had been only seconds—she fell to her knees in front of him and took his face in her palms. "Duncan. Duncan, can you hear me?"

Her only hope was that her father had been in a hurry when he took Duncan's mind, and she would be able to reach him before it was too late.

CHAPTER 22

Duncan heard a voice far off in the distance. A voice he recognized. He strained to hear it again over the taunts of his tormentors, fighting the bonds that held him. When it faded away, he cried out, unable to think past the pain, knowing he would never hear the voice again.

And then he did.

Melodic and sweet, it called to him like the morning song of a bird, awakening something deep inside of him and pulling it upward out of the hell he burned in.

Claws and teeth tore at his skin as the horrendous things they chanted grew louder in his ears.

His wolf huddled deep within him, afraid, as hands gripped his cock and balls, rubbing him raw, forcing him to respond as things were done to him. Sick things. Horrendous things. Things he never would've thought were possible.

Duncan felt himself sinking into the terrifying quagmire

of his own mind. A very small part of him knew that's all it was. It was all in his head. But the larger part of him felt everything, suffered everything, and knew he would never escape this hell again.

Through the haze of noise and heat, something soft touched his jaw and he caught a whiff of primrose.

But that couldn't be. There were no flowers here. Only the stench of rotting flesh.

The voice came to him again. Barely rising above the others. Calling his name. It faded in and out of the growled slurs and foul language, a dapple of sunlight dancing through the tree branches to warm his soul.

Something soft and wet touched his lips and instinctively he tried to turn his head away. It took him a moment to realize it wasn't the rough, sandpaper texture of a swollen tongue.

They were lips, soft and sweet, and they were kissing him.

Desperate to get away from the repulsive mouths licking and sucking every inch of skin on his body, he forced himself to focus on those lips and those lips alone.

He knew those lips. Knew that taste.

His wolf flicked its tail and pricked its ears.

"Duncan, come back to me. Stay with me. No one else is here. It's only you and I."

"Yer wrong," he told the sweet voice. His voice caught on a sob. "Yer wrong. I can hear them. I can see them. Och." The breath he inhaled was ragged. "I can *feel* them."

"No," the voice whispered against his lips. "No, wolf. It's

only us. You only hear me. You only see me. You only feel me."

He tried. Truly, he did.

"Fight them, Duncan. You need to fight them. I can't do it for you."

For a long time, forever it seemed, he reached for her, only to be torn away and beaten down by fists and claws and repulsive words. His stomach revolted at their touch and tears wet his cheeks. Violated and ashamed, he recoiled from the demons, pulling into himself until he could no longer hear their gravel voices or feel the burn of their tongues and teeth.

"No! No, Duncan, come back. You have to come back to me or I'll lose you." Something soft touched his ear. "And I'm not going to lose you! Do you hear me, wolf? You have to come back."

The salty scent of tears filled his nose. So strong he could smell it over the rot. His own? He didn't know. Something warm and tender touched his chest, and he couldn't control the cry of pain as it stroked over his raw skin with feather-light touches. But *och*, he ached so for that touch and did not want it to stop. Not ever. Not even when it traveled down his stomach to his cock.

"No! No! Dinna touch me!" he cried. But she ignored him, and suddenly that tender touch was wrapped around him, easing the soreness there.

And then the touch changed. Hot and wet, it stroked him with soft caresses, chasing away everything but the feelings...

Duncan groaned and closed his eyes. His hands buried themselves in silky curls. A shudder wracked his body as the pain ebbed away to be replaced by pleasure. Cool, damp air caressed his raw skin. He could no longer feel the burn of the hands and teeth and tongues that handled him like something without care or feelings.

Sweet lips moved up his torso, kissing away the pain and fears. A soft voice whispered loving things in his ear. Sexy things. Things that made him growl with hunger instead of cringe with fear and disgust.

"Come back to me, Duncan. I need you."

Slowly, he opened his eyes to a rainbow of colors that lit up a wee, bonnie face surrounded by a fall of dark curls. "Ryanne?"

A watery smile was his response. "It's okay. You're here with me. It was all in your mind."

He wanted to believe her.

"Do you remember where you are?"

Aye, he remembered.

The colors dimmed in her eyes, replaced by worry and fear as they searched his face. "It's not real, Duncan. None of that was real."

"You were there," he murmured.

"Yes. I'm sorry. I had to. It was the only way to pull you back."

"What did you see?" he asked her. He needed to know how much of that she had witnessed.

"It doesn't matter."

"It matters tae me."

She shook her head. "Tricks of the Fae. Horrifying and repulsive. But that's all it was. They weren't really there. Nothing was true except me."

He studied the lass in front of him. His hands were still buried in her hair, and when he went to move them to her face, he saw they were trembling. Still, he touched her, wanting to know she was real and this wasn't some new horror he was experiencing. "I need tae kiss ye."

"I need to kiss you, too," she told him. "I've never been so scared, Duncan, as when I walked in here and saw you in the throes of a nightmare created solely by my father. I didn't know how I was going to pull you out."

He didn't know either, but somehow, she had. And she'd done it by coming into the nightmare with him.

His wolf prowled restlessly just beneath the surface of his skin, and Duncan growled low in his throat.

Colors flickered in Ryanne's eyes. "Kiss me, Duncan. I need to feel you, and I think you need the same."

He wanted to, he did. "I dinna trust it, lass. I dinna trust ye are truly here."

So, she made the decision for him. Pulling his head down to hers, she took his mouth with a hunger that rivaled anything he had felt in his life or in his dreams.

With a moan, he took what he needed from her. What was true. The scent of her filled his nose, sweet primrose heavy with the musky notes of her arousal. Her hands stroked him everywhere she could reach with a soft urgency, wiping clean the last remnants of the nightmare he'd been under.

It was with surprise he realized he was still wearing the jeans he'd carried with him and hastily thrown on before coming into the cave. More proof that what he'd just gone through hadn't been real.

Ryanne's lips left his to move along his jaw and down his throat. He let his head fall back. Everywhere she touched was fire that burned him in the most pleasurable of ways. Duncan didn't feel the stone beneath the knees or the ache in his muscles, only the burning desire to slide deep inside of her and let the wet heat of her body soothe away the last traces of the prince's hallucination.

The heavy shirt she wore was too big and easy for him to work his hands beneath. The feel of her skin was heaven, the weight of her breasts a gift in his palms.

It wasn't enough.

She made an unhappy noise when he forced her to break their connection so he could pull the shirt up and off. He needed to see her.

But she did him one better.

Standing up, Ryanne kicked off her boots and tugged down her jeans, leaving everything in a pool of clothing on the rocks.

He reached out, touched the soft curls between her legs, then grabbed her by the hips and pulled her to his mouth. His fingers held her open as his tongue dove between the satiny folds to find the taste of her. Ryanne gripped his hair, pulling it near from his head as a long moan tore from her throat.

Och. He'd never tasted anything better than this female.

Duncan loved her with his mouth until she came on his tongue, and then he did it again, and again, until she trembled in his hands and her legs could barely hold her up.

Her taste and scent were all over him, completely erasing what had happened before. When she was crying out his name over and over—part plea for him to stop and part begging he never did—he sat back on his heels and yanked her down so she was straddling his lap. Quickly, he pushed his jeans down and gripped his cock with one hand. He was thick and hard for her. "Come onto me, Ryanne. I need tae be inside ye."

Hands on his shoulders, she lifted enough so he could line himself up at her entrance. "Now, lass. Take me now."

Her eyes on his, she took him into her sweet heat. Her mouth fell open on a gasp as he filled her. She was tight and hot and wet and the best thing Duncan had ever felt.

"I fear I can no' last long," he said through gritted teeth. Not when she felt so good and he needed her so very much.

Pieces of things best left forgotten tried to penetrate the fog of his lust, and for a moment he froze, lost in the horrors of the past and present.

She must have known, for suddenly she was there, wrapped around his body in the physical world and with him in his mind in the ethereal one. With whispered words in his head and the clasp of her body around him, she brought him back until it was only her and the pleasure rocketing down his spine and into his balls until he swelled so tight within her he didn't know how he still fit.

Pulling her tight to him, Duncan came inside of her with

such force his muscles tensed painfully and his wolf tore at his gut.

When he could speak, he dropped his head to her shoulder. "Dinna move, lass," he begged her between ragged breaths. "I need a moment."

Her arms wrapping around his shoulders was the best thing he'd ever felt. Even more so than the coupling that had just occurred.

Duncan had never felt the things he was feeling at that very moment. His insides were warm and gooey, and yet at the same time, he felt a near violent possession for this female in his arms. He knew in that moment he would kill anyone who tried to part them.

He also knew he would never be able to give her as much as she'd given him. "Thank ye," he whispered. "For pulling me out o' that place."

"I want to do one better," she told him.

"What's that?"

"I want to try to take it away completely. The memories of those things."

Pulling back, he caught her eyes with his. "I do no' want ye tae do that, although I appreciate th' thought."

She frowned. "You don't have to be scared. I've never done it before, but I've never gone there to help someone before, either. And I think I know what to do to help you forget."

"I dinna want tae forget, lass. I want tae remember it all."

"I don't understand," she said after a pause.

He pushed a wayward curl away from her face. "I dinna

want ye tae do it because I don't ever want tae forget what it is you've done for me. I will no' ever be able tae repay ye, but if ye will let me, I would like tae try."

She gave him a strange look and opened her mouth to say something when Duncan heard someone entering the cave. Quickly covering her mouth with his hand, he gave her a tight shake of his head. When he was certain she understood, he lifted her from his lap and handed her her shirt. As she slipped it over her head, he got to his feet and secured his pants.

Raising his nose, he sniffed the air. Immediately, he relaxed, but still pushed Ryanne behind him to hide her near nakedness. "Och, Cedric! Ye need tae stop doing this!"

His alpha appeared, and he was as naked as the day he was born, his black hair hanging loose over his shoulders. He took in the situation at a glance and grinned. "It's no my fault ye both are goin' at it every time I turn around." When he neared, he peeked around Duncan's shoulder to smile at Ryanne. "Excuse my bare arse."

Duncan growled his displeasure, but Cedric paid no mind.

"Where is th' prince?"

"He's no' here." As Ryanne found her pants and shoes and pulled them on, he filled Cedric in on everything that had happened, skimming over the details of how Ryanne had saved him. Again.

Cedric bared his teeth, but Duncan had the feeling it was less directed at him than at what had happened to him. "I told Brock tae keep ye at home. Yer a weak link when it comes tae the prince, Duncan. He kens how tae get tae ye, and I might not always be there tae save ye."

"If I may point it out, ye were no' there this time, Cedric, and everything worked out."

Cedric crossed his arms. "Aye. Ye were lucky Brock and I were there tae help yer lass, or it would no' have."

Ryanne stepped around him. "So, my father left Duncan here and thinks I'm dead. Again. That will work to my advantage when I confront him this time."

Duncan spun around to face her. Gripping her upper arms, he shook his head. "No, Ryanne. I will no' let ye go after yer father again. Th' next time ye verra well may not get away."

She stiffened under his hands. "I don't recall asking your permission, wolf."

His upper lip lifted in a snarl. "Ye will no' risk yer life just tae settle th' score. I will take care o' the prince."

"Och. Haud yer wheesht!" Cedric told them. "The both o' ye! Neither o' ye are doing anything. As a matter o' fact, I think ye should both lay low for a while."

"That's not acceptable to me," Ryanne told him.

Cedric speared her with the "look". Duncan knew that look. And although she couldn't feel the weight of the alpha's will as he could, Duncan knew she would not be getting what she wanted.

Not yet.

"I ken that, Ryanne," Cedric told her. "But if ye want tae stop yer father, I think yer going tae need help. And I happen tae ken a few wolves and Faeries who would be willing tae do just that."

Mimicking his stubborn pose, she turned her face, refusing to look at him.

Cedric looked to Duncan for help.

"Ryanne." Gently, he took her hand and turned her toward him. "Will ye agree tae just step back for a short time and let Cedric come up with a plan. If ye dinna think it will work, and with my alpha's permission, I will help ye take out th' prince."

"I can agree tae that," Cedric said.

She stared at him for a long time. "Okay," she finally agreed.

Cedric clapped his hands together. "Now that we are all in accord, Brock is pulling around th' Jeep. How aboot we all go home and fill everyone in, then figure out where we're going tae put th' two o' ye where th' prince will no' find ye."

Tucking a curl behind her ear, Duncan gave her a smile. She returned it with a hesitant one of her own.

EPILOGUE

B ack at the home of the wolves, showered, changed and rested. Ryanne was introduced to the other wolves she hadn't met yet, including their mates—Heather, Bronaugh, Bitsy, and Keelin.

The Key.

The other Faeries greeted her with differing levels of friendliness. Heather being the nicest and Bronaugh eyeing her with suspicion.

Between her, Duncan, and Cedric, they filled in the others on everything that had happened. Without a word between them, they left out parts about Duncan no one needed to know. Those things were personal and not essential to the story. At least not now.

The others agreed she and Duncan should go into hiding. At least, temporarily. And Ryanne had to grudgingly agree with their logic. The others would act like everything was as it always was with the prince. They would put on a show "searching" for Duncan, while they regrouped and tried to figure out Prince Nada's next move.

Not an easy task with a Faerie as ancient and powerful as him.

As Cedric and the others were filing out, Duncan's pack brothers each came over and slapped him on the arm and shoulder as their females gave him quick hugs.

All except Keelin. Her male kept her close to his side as he eyed Duncan with distrust.

"I need to talk to you," Ryanne told her.

"I know," she told her with a smile. "Later."

Ryanne nodded, and Keelin gave her a quick kiss on the cheek before turning away to say goodbye to Duncan.

Despite the visible aggression toward him from her mate, Duncan gave her a saucy wink and a big grin. "Dinna let this one get tae ye," he told her. "He only does that because he kens he is no' worthy o' ye."

She grinned back. "This is true." Then with a final wave, she and her grumbly wolf left, leaving Ryanne and Duncan alone.

Ryanne had watched this exchange and the others with interest, until she finally realized what that feeling was inside of her. The one that ripped at her insides and made her want to cry in the corner and kill everyone in sight all at the same time.

She was envious.

Duncan turned back to her. When his eyes met hers, she caught the last remnants of the grin he offered to others. The one that offered fun and sex and butterfly flutters in one's stomach. But as always, when he looked at her it slowly faded away.

Heat crept up the back of her neck, and she looked away. She felt more than saw Duncan step in closer to her.

"Ryanne? Lass, what's wrong?"

Feeling like a fool, she wasn't going to say anything. She was a grown female and didn't have the time or the need for all of this frivolous behavior. Didn't need the attention of another to make her feel good about herself.

Didn't need it. But she wanted it. From him. "Why don't you ever flirt with me like that?" Somehow, she found the nerve to meet his eyes.

His brows lowered in confusion. "What?"

"You never flirt with me," she repeated. Stronger now. "Every other female who looks your way gets a wink and a smile. A teasing comment or a compliment. And I'm just wondering, why don't I? Am I not attractive to you? Am I not fun?"

He stared at her in confusion for a long time. It was so long, in fact, she began to wonder if she'd actually said all that out loud or just thought it in her head.

She rubbed the spot between her eyebrows, trying to relieve the sudden pressure. Perhaps it had been a stupid thing to ask, as the answer was quite obvious.

"Ryanne, look at me, lass."

Reluctantly, she dropped her arm back down to her side and did as he asked.

Duncan was still staring down at her, but his green eyes were both bright and intense. His expression dead serious.

"I dinna flirt with ye because yer no' like those others." He kept his distance even now, after everything.

She barely kept herself from snorting. "That's quite obvious, thank you." Then she gave him a tight smile, fighting the pain rising within her until she could get somewhere alone to process it.

"No, ye dinna understand what I'm saying."

Her emotions were spun tight, and she may have shouted at him. "Then what exactly are you saying, wolf?"

Gently, never taking his burning green eyes from her face, he took her hands in both of his. "I dinna flirt with ye, lass, because ye are...ye are..." His brows lowered, his eyes searching her face. "Because ye are more, Ryanne. I can no' explain it."

"Can you try?" Her voice sounded tiny and unsure in her own ears.

With a deep breath and a nod, he seemed to brace himself. Against what? she wondered.

"I act th' way I do with females, with other females," he corrected himself. "Because it was what I did, ye ken, after."

He didn't have to explain to her what event he was speaking of. And now she knew why the steel had suddenly infused his spine. He assumed that posture whenever he had to speak of what was done to him.

"I don't even remember when it started, but it made me feel...more a male, somehow, by making th' females feel good in th' only way I could. Do ye ken what I'm sayin'?"

Her wolf stood before her, proud and strong, but there

was nevertheless a vulnerability in his eyes that tugged hard on her heart.

"But with ye, Ryanne, I can no' do it. I can no' pretend with ye. Because ye are *more*." Releasing one of her hands, he brushed his fingers down her cheek and along her jaw. "Ye are *more*. Tis th' only way I ken how tae say it."

"Oh," she said.

Oh.

One side of his mouth turned up, and she watched in fascination as a dimple appeared. "I'd verra much like tae kiss ye now. If that's alright with ye."

In the center of her chest, her heart began to pump loud and hard.

She was more.

His hand cupped her face as he leaned down and touched his forehead to hers. "Och, Ryanne. I never want tae be without ye, lass," he whispered.

And as he claimed her lips, she felt the touch of his soul to hers, and she knew.

He was *more*.

And he was hers.

* * *

Thank you for reading! I hope you loved Duncan and Ryanne's story. The next book in The Kincaid Werewolves series is
The Alpha's Surrender.
Cedric would give his life for the safety of this pack.

But he soon learns it would be far more painful to give up his heart.

The Faerie prince wants Cedric to mate with Duana, but she has neither the time nor the inclination to "date". Especially not a mangy alpha wolf who scorches her body with his white-hot eyes and turns her insides to mush with his Scottish brogue.

READ THE ALPHA'S SURRENDER NOW

ABOUT THE AUTHOR

L.E. Wilson writes romance starring intense alpha males and the women who are fearless enough to tame them — for the most part anyway. ;) In her novels you'll find smoking hot scenes, a touch of suspense, some humor, a bit of gore, and multifaceted characters, all working together to combine her lifelong obsession with the paranormal and her love of romance.

Her writing career came about the usual way: on a dare from her loving husband. Little did she know just one casual suggestion would open a box of worms (or words as the case may be) that would forever change her life.

Lattes and music are a necessary part of her writing

process, though sometimes you'll find her typing away at her favorite Starbucks. She walks two miles to get there, to make up for all of those coffees.

On a Personal Note:

"I love to hear from my readers! Contact me anytime at le@lewilsonauthor.com."

Keep In Touch With L.E.
lewilsonauthor.com
le@lewilsonauthor.com

Made in the USA
Middletown, DE
15 August 2021